CLAIMED BY
THE WEALTHY
MAGNATE

CLAIMED BY THE WEALTHY MAGNATE

BY

NINA MILNE

First published in Great Britain 2017
By Mills & Boon, an imprint of HarperCollins*Publishers*
1 London Bridge Street, London, SE1 9GF

Large Print edition 2017

© 2017 Nina Milne

ISBN: 978-0-263-07141-2

Printed and bound in Great Britain
by CPI Antony Rowe, Chippenham, Wiltshire

To all things Venice!

CHAPTER ONE

LADY KAITLIN DERWENT, poster girl for the aristocracy, daughter of the Duke and Duchess of Fairfax, stared at her nigh on unrecognisable reflection and wondered if she'd run mad... No, she *knew* she must have run mad.

There could be no other explanation for the fact that she was standing in this glitzy Barcelona hotel room, her Titian-red hair obscured under a bottleful of cheap blonde dye, her green eyes masked by baby-blue contact lenses, on a 'Blonde Hair and Blue Eyes in Barcelona' themed hen weekend for a woman she hadn't seen for years.

'You OK?' Lynette Cooper, her childhood playmate and the bride-to-be, leant forward to peer more closely into the dressing table mirror and layered on another sheen of letterbox-red lipstick. 'Are you sure you won't come out tonight? We're making cocktails and then we're drinking cocktails.'

Kaitlin summoned a smile. 'No, thank you. I appreciate it, but I'd be gatecrashing.'

She didn't know any of the other guests; it had been a crazy impulse of the type she never, *ever* demonstrated to ask Lynette if she could join the hen group so that she could escape for a weekend. Travel as part of a group with a degree of anonymity and gain some time out, some space to think.

'I will truly be happy chilling out here. I'll order room service, watch a film and go to sleep.'

Lynette tipped her blonde head to one side. 'You sure?'

'I'm sure.'

'OK.' Lynette's smile was genuine, and so reminiscent of her ten-year-old self that Kaitlin couldn't help but smile back.

'And, Lynette... Thank you.'

'You're welcome, Kaitlin. I know we've lost touch, but I'm glad I could help. Really.'

Lynette looked as though she wanted to say more, and Kaitlin knew she needed to forestall her. She wouldn't explain the reasons for the breakdown of their friendship all those years ago—*couldn't* revisit the memories of a trauma she had relegated to the surreal.

'And I am really grateful, Lynette. Now, go and have fun. Don't worry about me.'

Lynette stood, undecided, and then nodded. 'OK. Be good. Call me if you change your mind and want to meet up with us.'

With that she swirled from the room in a gust of perfume.

Be good. No problem there. Lady Kaitlin Derwent was always good—never a breath of scandal to her name and that was the way it would stay. This was as mad as she was ever likely to be—disguised as a blonde, holed up in a hotel room in Barcelona, so that she could contemplate her future.

The recent conversation with her parents pounded her temples.

Her mother's voice, warm with honey. Yet it was a warmth all the Derwent children knew to be false. 'Kaitlin. We have good news. Prince Frederick of Lycander is looking for a bride. We think you fit the bill.'

The Duke of Fairfax had snorted. 'We know

you do, and we expect you to do everything in your power to ensure it is you who joins him at the altar. Royal blood and Derwent blood joined in alliance.'

The Duchess had looked at her with something as near to approval as she ever showed, eyed her up and down and nodded her ash-blonde head. 'So it shall be.'

Her parents had spoken and Kaitlin had smiled her cool, poised, serene smile—one of many practised in front of the mirror until her cheek muscles ached. 'I'll do my best.'

Now, sitting on the single bed of the Barcelona hotel room, Kaitlin closed her eyes and wondered what on earth she was doing here. What was the point of contemplation? There was nothing to muse over. After all, her future had been mapped out, her destiny already determined. Granted, it was a future most women would kill for—a guarantee of wealth and a young handsome sovereign prince to go with it.

A glance out of the window showed the dusky Barcelona evening. The breeze carried in staccato bursts of chatter, the smell of heat-hazed streets and a hint of sangria. Another glance at the mirror reassured her that her own siblings wouldn't recognise her.

Well, Cora might, with her twin's intuition, but Gabriel certainly wouldn't. A familiar pang of guilt touched her at the thought of Cora—at the knowledge that her relationship with her sister had lost any semblance of closeness. As for Gabriel—right now she didn't even know where her brother was. The future Duke of Fairfax had disappeared on a prolonged sojourn abroad, leaving behind a supposedly jilted girlfriend and no indication of when he would return.

The Derwent siblings—on the surface they had it all, but in reality…

The impetus of emotion made her decision for her—pent-up energy roiled inside her, making the room's confines too restrictive, and instinct propelled her to the door, out of the room and down the carpeted stairs towards the lobby.

But as she looked around at the bustle in the marble foyer, the people all strangers, a tsunami of panic welled inside her without warning. Alarm and anxiety crashed in as they hadn't for—oh, so many years.

Fool that she was.

This had been a mistake. She should never have come here—never have set foot out of her carefully planned life trajectory. At best she should at least have remained in the safety of her room. She needed to retrace her steps. If only her legs would co-operate. Dots danced in front of her eyes and her lungs refused to work.

A last vestige of common sense had her leaning against a marble pillar in the hope of obscurity...

Daniel Harrington stepped out of the elevator into the hotel lobby. Feelings of futile anger mixed with equally pointless hurt banded his chest.

Stupidity incarnate.

Who knew what had possessed him to attempt a reunion with his family? Ten years ago they had turned their backs on him, refused to countenance his decision to go legitimate, to no longer turn a blind eye.

'If you walk out of that door, Danny, you don't get to come back. Ever. You will be dead to us.'

That walk had been the hardest choice he'd ever made. But he'd done it, and he'd been a fool to think there would be any softening now. So he had only himself to blame for this wasted journey. But he had hoped that his mother, at least, would relent, would want to see her eldest son.

Instead his stepfather had sent his deputy in her stead—a man who had delivered his message with a cruelty that had exercised Daniel's self-restraint to the utmost.

As he strode towards the revolving doors, the message echoed in his ears.

'Ghosts get no visitors. Dead is dead, Danny boy. Dead is for ever, and you are dead to the Rosso family.'

He nearly missed the movement that had caught at the edge of his vision.

Dyed blonde hair caught back in a messy ponytail, blue eyes filled with anguish… The woman leant against a marble pillar that mostly concealed her from the guests that dotted the foyer. Her breath rasped in heaving gasps that indicated a full-scale panic attack.

With an abrupt turn Daniel veered off and halted in front of her. 'Are you OK?'

Stupid question, but the words seemed at least

to steady her slightly, and she blinked her eyes in rapid succession.

'I'm fi…' she began, then gasped out a half-laugh. 'No, I'm not.'

Daniel gestured to a concierge. 'Water, please.' Turning, he held an arm out to the woman. 'Let me help you. You need to sit down.'

'Thank you.'

He watched as she visibly pulled herself together, almost as if through sheer will power. Her breathing was still ragged, but no longer desperate as she pushed away from the fluted column and stood with one hand resting on it.

'I'll be fine.' She nodded her thanks to the hotel staff member who came over with a bottle of water. 'Really.'

'Is there someone I can call or get for you? Or…?'

'No!' The syllable was a touch too sharp. 'Really, I'm fine now. Thank you for your help.'

'I've hardly helped.'

He studied her for a long moment, saw the vulnerability still in her eyes, along with an anxiety she was clearly doing her best to mask.

'But I'd like to. How about I buy you a drink? Stay with you until I'm sure you're OK?'

Surprise touched with an understandable wariness etched a frown on her face.

'No, thank you.' The words were polite but final. 'I don't drink with strangers.'

'And *I* don't leave damsels in distress on their own in hotel lobbies. We can have a drink here. In the public bar, full of plenty of people. If you're in trouble maybe I can help you.'

'What makes you think I'm in trouble?'

Daniel shrugged. 'Instinct. I'm a lawyer. Lots of my clients are in trouble. You get to know the signs.'

'Well, in this case you've misread the signals. I appreciate your concern, but I'm not in trouble and I don't need any more help than you've already given me.'

The words, though softly spoken, were uttered with determination, and Daniel knew he should go on his currently less than merry way. But his instincts were usually bang on the button, and the idea that this woman was in dire straits of some sort persisted.

Not his business. Though there was more to it

than that. Dammit, she was beautiful. Wide blue eyes were fringed with thick dark lashes and un-enhanced by make-up. A few tendrils of blonde hair had escaped the ponytail and framed a clas-sically oval face. Slender and long-legged, she held herself with a poise and grace that added distinction to her beauty.

As if made uncomfortable by his scrutiny, she shifted from foot to foot and turned her head slightly to one side.

'If you don't need my help then perhaps we could just enjoy each other's company? You wouldn't think it to look at me, but I am a scin-tillating conversationalist.'

He accompanied the words with a wriggle of his eyebrows and to his surprise, and perhaps hers, her lips curved up into a smile. Though she still her shook her head.

'Humour me. One drink. So I can be sure you are OK. You can ask the staff to keep an eye on us, if you're worried. In fact I think they al-ready are.'

The smile vanished and her eyes shaded with a hint of anxiety as she glanced round to where the concierge still watched them.

'OK. One drink.'

He held out a hand. 'I'm Daniel.'

The woman hesitated a moment before reaching her hand out to his. 'Lynette.'

Half an hour later, seated across from Daniel in the cool anonymity of the elegant yet highly functional hotel bar, Kaitlin sipped the last of her pomegranate cooler. The non-alcoholic blend of sweet and sour was exactly what she'd needed to revive her.

Come on, Kaitlin.

It wasn't the beverage, nor the comfort of the cream-cushioned round-backed seats, nor even the vivid splash of bright yellow flower arrangements—it was the man.

Daniel lacked her brother's classic handsomeness—the slight crook to his nose indicated that it might well have been broken once, and his features were craggy rather than aquiline—but in sheer presence he could rival Gabriel, even if the latter *was* the Earl of Wycliffe.

He projected a raw energy—a force that showed in the intense blue of his eyes, the jut of his jaw, the sheer focus he bestowed on her.

It was a focus underlain with a pull of attraction that caused a warning bell to toll in the dim recesses of her brain that knew the sheer scale of the stupidity of all this.

Attraction was a tug she couldn't afford to feel—an emotion that in truth she had never felt. The blight, she assumed, was a result of her childhood trauma.

Stop, Kaitlin. Don't go there.

The kidnap was an experience she had done her best to suppress, and she had every intention of keeping it buried in the deepest, darkest depths of her psyche, never to surface. After all she had created her safe, controlled Lady Kaitlin persona to achieve that exact obliteration of her memory banks.

'Another drink?' he asked, and his deep voice caressed her skin like velvet and decadent chocolate. 'Or how about dinner?'

'Thank you.'

But no—they were the words she knew she should say. Each minute she spent with Daniel increased the risk of recognition, the possibility that she would slip up and reveal her true identity. That would be a disaster—her parents would be incoherent with anger if Lady Kaitlin Derwent was revealed to have been picked up by a stranger in a Barcelona bar. Because—and she might as well face it—if she agreed to dinner this would no longer be a 'medical' interlude. It would move into different territory altogether. An unfamiliar minefield of a terrain. So...

'But I don't want to disrupt your plans. I'm fine now. Thank you for coming to my rescue.'

'I have no plans.' There was a bleak note in his voice under the casual disclaimer.

'You must have had *some* plans,' she countered. 'You were on your way somewhere when you ran into me.'

'Nowhere specific. Wherever the night took me.'

His shoulders lifted and her gaze snagged on their breadth. Once again awareness struck—an undercurrent that swirled between them across the square glass-topped table.

'So what do you say?'

'I...I shouldn't.'

'Why not?' Ice-blue eyes met hers. 'Is anyone else expecting you?'

'No.'

'So you're here alone?'

Kaitlin hesitated...couldn't face the complications involved in a full explanation. And, anyway, to all intents and purposes she was alone. 'Yes.'

'You're sure?'

'Yes.'

'Then how about dinner? No strings. We're two people alone in a vibrant city and I could do with some company.'

The words held a ring of truth, and for a moment she wondered what demons he wanted to hold at bay.

Temptation warred with the final grains of common sense, which pointed out that after all she had to eat.

His shoulders lifted in a shrug. 'I had a reservation at one of Barcelona's best restaurants—I could try and resurrect it.'

Kaitlin frowned. 'So you *did* have plans?'

'Let's say my plans didn't materialise.'

An underlying harshness coated the words and pain flashed across those blue eyes.

Kaitlin hesitated, sensing that the man opposite her was hurting. Clearly he'd been stood up.

Doubt unfurled—somehow that didn't seem a possibility. It wasn't a scenario that played true.

Ridiculous. Yes, he was good-looking and magnetic and…and… But she hardly knew him or his relationship background.

Yet more reasons to make her exit now.

But she didn't want to. Never again would she have a chance like this. To be free, to shed the 'Lady Kaitlin' persona. Because soon there would be the meeting with Prince Frederick of Lycander—a meeting at which she needed to demonstrate her suitability to be a Lycander bride and then…

Enough. She wouldn't—couldn't think of that now.

'Dinner sounds wonderful. A night of freedom before I step into a gilded cage.'

Oh, hell. She'd said the words out loud. and now this stranger looked at her with a sharpness, an intensity she couldn't fathom. Almost as if it were someone else he saw, not her.

'Never voluntarily step into a cage you don't have a key to unlock.'

The words had an edge—a meaning she needed to deflect. Tonight she didn't want to think about the marriage that awaited her—a marriage that she had believed she wanted. An alliance...a safe future and a role she would excel in.

'I'll bear it in mind.' She turned her lips up into her Lady Kaitlin smile—friendly yet deflecting. 'Now, I'd prefer to think about dinner. But there's no need for Barcelona's best restaurant.' That was Lady Kaitlin's milieu. 'Let's just walk and see where the night takes us.'

Innate caution pointed out that this man was a stranger—instinct told her she could trust him, but she knew all too well the follies of trust and a tendril of panic unfurled.

Think.

'In the meantime, before we go, I'm going to call a friend and tell her I'll be checking in every hour.'

No need to tell Lynette that she was having dinner with a stranger; instead she'd say she was walking alone and would feel better if she could check in.

'Works for me.'

'I'll be back in a minute.'

To Kaitlin's relief Lynette didn't make a big

deal of the situation—she seemed to accept that Kaitlin never travelled alone and that the aristocracy were ultra-security-conscious.

And so ten minutes later she and Daniel stepped out of the hotel's revolving doors into the hustle and bustle of the Barcelona street.

Instinctively Kaitlin halted, almost overwhelmed by the sheer buzz that emanated from the throngs of chattering people. Her gaze darted to the street performers who plied their expertise for the amusement of passers-by. The scents of garlic and chilli and spices wafted from the numerous tapas bars that dotted the early medieval streets and overflowed with evening revellers.

'You OK?'

Kaitlin pushed her shoulders back and nodded. Panic would *not* ruin this evening. The old dormant fear that coloured her every move, that made her live her life bound by rules and regulations and routine, would be suspended tonight. No one knew her identity; no one had any interest in snatching her now.

'I'm fine. It's just so vibrant it stopped me in my tracks.'

Yet instinct had her walking close to his reassuring warmth—logical or not, she sensed that Daniel would keep her safe. Perhaps it was the confident, swagger-free, don't-mess-with-me aura he projected, or the sheer lithe muscular strength in each step. Whatever it was, it worked, and as they walked Kaitlin relaxed, absorbed the sights, the awe-inspiring grand patchwork of architectural styles that graced the skyline, where dark Gothic façades neighboured the harlequin buildings of the Modernistas.

But it wasn't only the Barcelona experience that she absorbed—as they walked her whole body hummed with an awareness of Daniel... Something shimmered and sizzled in the air between them, exacerbated by the occasional brush of their hands or the press of their bodies against each other in the crowds. Each touch sent heat through her, caused her tummy to loop the loop.

Even more head-spinning was the knowledge that he felt the same way; she could sense it—see it in the hunger of his blue gaze when it rested on her.

Some space, time out, seemed a good idea, so she could make an attempt to process the enormity of her reactions. 'Shall we eat?' she suggested pointing to a tapas bar. 'That one looks as good as any.'

'Sure.'

She followed him into the dimly lit packed interior and watched as he managed to snag one of the few small square tables covered in plastic red and white checked tablecloths.

As they looked around she realised where they were. 'It's a *pintxo* bar. I've never been in one— but I think they originate from the Basque region of Spain.'

He nodded. 'Basically *pintxos* are mouth-sized tapas—always skewered with toothpicks. We just go up to the bar, help ourselves and tuck in. We keep the toothpicks and at the end we pay by the number of toothpicks.'

Kaitlin eyed the throng of people at the bar, most of them standing and eating, chatting and drinking with abandon. She knew that even with the new-found freedom of being 'Lynette' she couldn't risk it. Not the possibility of another panic attack brought on by the crowd or that of being recognised.

Daniel looked at her with a glint of amusement. 'I can go and get a selection for us both.'

'Thank you. That would be kind.' Perhaps a touch too much aristocratic hauteur in her voice there, and she eased it with a smile. 'I'll order the drinks.'

Ten minutes later he returned to the table. 'Here we go.'

'Delicious. Ham *empanadillas*, *sobrassada* sausage with honey, apple and crispy Idiazabal cheese *pintxos* made of chicken, tempura with saffron mayonnaise, melted *provolone* with mango and ham, and a mini-*brochette* of pork.'

'That's an impressive Spanish accent. I take it you speak the language?'

'A little.' The Duchess had ensured Kaitlin was fluent in a number of languages.

'You must be prepared, Kaitlin, should you marry into European aristocracy.'

'As part of your job?'

'No. I work in an art gallery.' No harm in sharing *that* fact; lots of people worked in art galleries, after all.

He speared a *pinxto* and surveyed her thoughtfully. 'So, are you here on business? Barcelona has plenty of art.'

Kaitlin shook her head. 'This trip is personal.'

'Are you in trouble?'

The unexpectedness of the question caused her to tense, and a drop of sangria slopped over the edge of her glass and hit the wooden table. Placing her glass down carefully, Kaitlin mopped up the red liquid with a napkin, watching the cloth absorb the ruby stain.

'We had this conversation earlier and I said no.'

'I know you did. I'm not sure I believe you.'

'I'm not in trouble. I came to Barcelona because I needed some space. Tonight I want to forget the past and the future and live in the present.'

An arrested expression flickered across his face in the candlelit alcove. 'A night of freedom?' he said, quoting her words from earlier.

'Yes.'

Daniel raised his glass. 'To your night of freedom.'

His blue eyes met hers and what she saw shot a funny little thrill through her and she stilled. The sheer unfamiliarity of the sensation made her light-headed, made her dizzy with its intensity, and her body felt energised as every nerve-end tingled in anticipation.

The hours danced by, and the air was tinged with motes of awareness as they talked of everything and nothing. By mutual unspoken consent the conversation veered away from the personal, so they discussed music, films and philosophy. But every word was punctuated by a growing expectancy—a heady underlying responsiveness and a growing realisation of where the evening might end up.

Eventually they shared a dessert, a decadent dark chocolate concoction, and as she spooned up the last sumptuous bite she met his gaze, saw desire ignite in his eyes. Then gently he took the spoon from her suddenly nerveless fingers and placed it on the plate. The chink of metal on china rang loud in her ear.

Oh, so gently he reached out and ran his thumb across her lower lip. She gasped—a small, involuntary sound—at the potency of her own reaction. Sensation uncoiled in her tummy...a need she'd never felt before. Without thought she cupped his jaw, wondered at the feel of his six o'clock shadow. Then his lips descended to hers and the world seemed to stop.

There was the taste of coffee and chocolate, the whirling rush of need, and the intense, sweet pleasure that streamed through her veins and sent a tingling rush to every bit of her body. Never before had she felt like this.

He pulled back, his breathing ragged, and he looked at her with such intensity as he said her name. 'Lynette...'

It was a reminder that she had this night and this night only. Ideas swirled round her head. A touch of fear as to whether she *could* do this, however much she wanted to—and, dammit, she *wanted* to.

For one grim instant the image of her dark, bearded kidnapper splayed through her vision, and then she looked at Daniel and the picture faded, dissipated by the white-hot burn of desire.

'I think we should move this somewhere else.'

'Are you sure?'

She was so sure—because she knew that these feelings could never happen to Lady Kaitlin. Perhaps because of the horror of what had happened during the kidnap... Whatever the reason, it didn't matter. The fact remained that the odds were she would never feel like this again, and right now, caught in the sheer, dizzying sensual mesh of desire, Kaitlin knew she wanted this man. Against all reason it felt right. It could only be for one night, but so be it.

'Yes. I'm sure.'

CHAPTER TWO

Nine months later...

DANIEL HARRINGTON PAUSED on the threshold of the immense marquee, his ice-blue eyes scanning the wedding guests with ruthless disregard. One part of his brain registered the glorious elegance that graced the wedding reception of Gabriel Derwent, Earl of Wycliffe, heir to the Duke of Fairfax. The sumptuous drapes of organza, the glittering twinkle of the fairy lights and the splash of colour provided by the overhanging Chinese lanterns. The delicate scent of flowers pervaded the air—gloriosa and hyacinth, decked the canvas in lavish arrangements.

But in truth Daniel had no interest in the décor, and limited interest in the bride and groom. He was here for one reason and one reason only, and his eyes continued their systematic search, skipping over the rich, the famous and the ordinary on a quest to find Lady Kaitlin Derwent—sister to the groom, and the bride's maid of honour.

Earlier in the proceedings he'd watched her walk down the aisle amidst a bevy of brides-maids, all dressed in different jewel shades, a medley of beauty. But the only woman he'd been interested in was her, Lady Kaitlin, and as he'd studied her poised, graceful movements suspicion had begun the conversion process to confirmation.

Yet it was still nigh on impossible to believe that the poised Titian-haired beauty, clad in expensive designer teal-green, was the same woman he'd met nine months before in a Barcelona hotel. But as the hymns and the vows had resonated from the rafters of the picturesque medieval church his gaze had never once ceased its lingering on her beautiful features, and certainty had dawned.

Daniel had no doubt whatsoever that 'Lynette' and Katlin Derwent were one and the same.

Now, in the vast marquee that housed the reception party, he located her. Stood in a corner, deep in conversation with a tall blond man he knew to be Prince Frederick, ruler of the Principality of Lycander. Raw emotion slammed into his gut. Anger alongside the unwanted sting of desire and a primal instinct that yelled *mine*.

Instinctively he bunched his hands into fists.

Cool it, Dan. Violence no longer featured in his life as a solution, and initiating a brawl was not an option. After all, Prince Frederick was blameless in this whole sorry mess, and it shouldn't matter to Daniel that Kaitlin's hand rested on the Prince's forearm as she looked up at him.

Yet anger at her deception still pulsed in his veins. Along with the memory of his sense of loss and chagrin when he'd woken up in the swish Barcelona hotel to find no sign of the woman he'd shared such an amazing night with. Not so much as a blonde hair curled on the pillow had spoken of her presence. No strand or fibre of clothing. Just an elusive trace of her rose scent, and the ache in his body that had awoken him in the expectation of her still being beside him.

Then had come worry—heightened by the fact that it had been her first time…a fact she had refused to elaborate on or discuss. Had he mistaken the wonder of the night? Did she have regrets that her first experience had been with a stranger?

Then had come the conviction that she *was* in trouble. Hell, he'd even wondered if she'd been forced to leave. More fool him.

Anger burned cold under his control.

He allowed only the civilised approach—Daniel got what he wanted through law, order and fair negotiation. That had been his vow a decade ago, and he'd lived by those rules ever since.

Frustration tautened his sinews with the desire to lash out. He would not revert to type—would not embrace the ethos of his family. That was why he'd walked away ten years before, though the cost had been high.

A memory snaked into his brain: his mother's beautiful face, twisted in entreaty as she'd stretched out a pleading hand. *'Don't go, Danny. Please don't walk out through that door.'*

'Daniel.'

He swivelled in recognition of the well-modulated tones of Gabriel Derwent, groom and brother of the Lady Kaitlin.

'Glad you could make it.'

Gabriel smiled and Daniel blinked—the Earl radiated palpable happiness.

'Etta. This is Daniel Harrington—CEO of Harrington Legal, a new associate of my father's, and also a new patron of the Caversham Foundation.'

Daniel recognised the slight edge to Gabriel's voice and couldn't blame him. He'd negotiated an invitation to this wedding with the Duke of Fairfax, Gabriel's father, by dint of making a sizeable donation to the Derwent Manor restoration fund. When Gabriel had found out he'd called Daniel and explained that he wanted an additional price—a 'donation with a difference' to the Caversham Foundation, a charitable trust that helped troubled teenagers.

'Daniel, this is my wife—Etta.'

Pride and awe touched the syllables, and Etta positively beamed, her tawny eyes sparkling with joy.

Daniel searched his repertoire of happy wedding talk. 'Congratulations,' he mustered.

Though who knew for what? Marriage shackled you, created ties that would bind and link and imprison you. His own mother's marriage was proof of that.

'Thank you.' Gabriel studied his expression and his smile widened. 'Though I get the feeling you aren't a fan of marriage.'

'It's just not for me.'

Etta shook her head. 'Perhaps you haven't met the right woman.'

His gaze must have flicked across to Kaitlin for a fraction of a second, because Gabriel followed his line of sight and his forehead creased in a small frown.

Daniel thought rapidly. 'Though from what I've read it sounds as though your sister will follow in your footsteps shortly?'

Keep it casual.

'Perhaps,' Gabriel said, his frown deepening, almost as if he didn't like the idea.

'Why don't we introduce you?' Etta suggested.

Bingo. Not exactly the way he'd planned it— but Daniel was nothing if not versatile. 'Great.'

Gabriel strode towards where Kaitlin and the Prince were engrossed in conversation. Satisfaction brought a small, cold smile to Daniel's lips as he followed.

* * *

Kaitlin looked up at Prince Frederick and tried to suppress the all too familiar feelings of panic. *Chill out. Or chillax.* Or whatever the current phrase was. But she couldn't—despite the size of the marquee she felt hemmed in, and fear knotted her tummy into a tangle of panic. Which was nuts. She was standing next to royalty—how much safer could she be? The Prince would have strategically placed bodyguards everywhere.

Though you *could* argue that those bodyguards were only interested in the protection of the Prince—she'd no doubt be seen as collateral damage.

No, that wasn't fair. Frederick would care. Not because he loved her—he'd been upfront about that—but because he was a dutiful man. Or at least she thought he was—the Prince was even better than she was at keeping his true self under wraps.

Yet over the past months she'd learnt he had a moral code that meant he would protect her out of duty.

So she was safe. But, however many times her brain told her that, her nerves still fluttered with

an anxiety that increased daily—a throwback
to all those years ago when it had been her constant companion. If she was honest, the panic
had been on the up ever since her disastrous trip
to Barcelona nine months before.

Barcelona. Don't go there.

As for the panic—she'd tamed it once, and
she'd tame it again. All she had to do was *be*
Lady Kaitlin—be the calm, in control woman
she'd taught herself to be. The woman who could
produce suitable emotion on tap without feeling
a thing.

'We need to talk, Kaitlin. In private.'

Oh, hell. She knew exactly what Prince Frederick wanted to talk about—he wanted to propose and she just didn't want him to. Not yet.
Not ever, said a small, defiant voice that she
tuned out without compunction. This was what
she wanted—what most women would rip their
own arm off for. Marriage to a wealthy, handsome prince who also possessed the bonus of
a moral code. So *of course* she wanted him to
propose—but just not *now.*

'Yes, we do. But not here. This is Gabe and

Etta's day. I don't want us to overshadow it in any way.'

She'd been there and done that at her sister's wedding, and the guilt still pinged within her.

He raised an eyebrow. 'I don't think us having a conversation will overshadow Gabe's wedding. In truth, I don't think *anything* could overshadow this day for him. Gabe is a man in love.'

Frederick was right—though who would have thought it? Her big brother, nearly as big an emotional disaster zone as Kaitlin herself, had succumbed to the biggest emotion of all and fallen hook, line and sinker for Etta Mason.

'Even so…it is still their day. If we disappear to have a "private" conversation every reporter in the room will clock it.'

To say nothing of her parents. The Duke and Duchess of Fairfax were watching their eldest daughter like a pair of hawk-eagle hybrids.

The Prince frowned, and it was a relief to hear the deep sound of her brother's voice from behind her.

'Kait.'

She turned gracefully, smile in place to greet the euphoric bridegroom, and then she froze.

Her brain scrambled for purchase and her stomach nosedived as her eyes absorbed the identity of the man standing next to her brother. Surely she was in the throes of a hallucination? *Please let that be the case.* She'd take the prospect of insanity over reality in a heartbeat.

Pulling up every ounce of learned poise and ability to rise to any social occasion, she forced her jaw to remain clenched and prayed that no one could hear the accelerated pounding of her heart as she let her gaze rest on the man next to Gabe.

No doubt about it—it was Daniel.

Same dark brown hair, same raw energy that couldn't be concealed by the expensively tailored suit. Those oh-so-familiar ice-blue eyes met hers full-on and she could read the anger in their depths. An anger she didn't—couldn't—blame him for. After the most magical night imaginable she'd sneaked away into the chilly Barcelona dawn without so much as a by your leave. Worse, she had lied shamelessly about her identity.

What to do? What to do *now*?

There was zilch she could do—except hope that he wouldn't expose her. Yet even as her head reeled with the sheer horror of the situation, and its potential for disaster, her body betrayed her with a frisson of memory that prickled her skin.

'Sorry to interrupt,' Gabe said, though Kaitlin noted there was not so much as a hint of apology in his tone. 'But I wanted to introduce you to someone. Kaitlin, this is Daniel Harrington. He has made a generous contribution to the manor and is also linked with the Caversham Foundation.'

Mind racing, Kaitlin forced her lips to turn up in a polite smile with a touch of appreciation. Her years of careful practice in front of a mirror to perfect a smile for any occasion was coming in handy. Even as her brain seethed with tumult it tried to come to terms with the scale of the disaster.

'Pleased to meet you,' she said, her voice even as she held out one perfectly manicured hand, impressed to see that her fingers didn't so much as tremble. It was a shame the same couldn't be said of her insides. Then he clasped her hand in his, in the briefest of handshakes, and a funny little thrill raced through her bloodstream.

No! No! No! There could be no thrills of any sort—that was a complete non-starter. It was imperative to focus, to work out a way to end this whole scenario before her life imploded. In public.

'Likewise,' Daniel said, his voice silk-smooth and deadly as nightshade. 'I must admit I hoped to meet you today.' A smile utterly devoid of mirth turned up his lips. 'I'd like to discuss a project with you—I realise this is a big day for you, and you have lots of duties as maid of honour, but it will only take a few minutes.'

Kaitlin quelled the urge to cover her ears, close her eyes and hope that would equate to sudden invisibility. But that wasn't an option. Somehow Daniel had worked out her identity and he now had the ammunition to embroil her in a scandal. Worse it would impact not just herself, but Frederick as well—and that wasn't fair. True enough, technically Kaitlin had done nothing wrong—but her association with Frederick had begun near enough to that disastrous Barcelona night as would make no difference. To the press, at least.

This scenario was a nightmare. She had hoped—believed—that she would never see Daniel again, and here he was, requesting a few minutes of her time.

Who was she kidding? His words had been posed as a request, but his eyes were glacial, his jaw was set, and she knew if she didn't acquiesce he'd have no hesitation in forcing the issue.

'Of course,' she murmured. 'I'd be interested to hear what you have to say.'

The words fell from her lips automatically—she didn't want anyone to suspect how rattled she was. Lady Kaitlin Derwent didn't *do* rattled, and now was not the time to start.

'Well, there's no time like the present. Would anyone mind if I whisk Kaitlin off?'

Kaitlin blinked. That was not what she had in mind—she'd wanted time to think, regroup.

Prince Frederick glanced at her. 'It is entirely up to Kaitlin whether it is convenient for her to speak with you now.'

Etta glanced from Daniel to Kaitlin and back again. 'I don't need you to do anything but

44 CLAIMED BY THE WEALTHY MAGNATE

enjoy yourself. That's what I'm hoping *every-one* will do.'

Daniel smiled. 'I promise I'll keep the business talk to a minimum.'

'Make sure you do,' Etta said with a light laugh. 'Now, we had better mingle.'

Gabe twined an arm round his bride's waist and they smiled at each other—smiles that could only be described as goofy—and Kaitlin experienced a small pang of envy, felt the sudden ache of emptiness. Exacerbated as she glanced from Frederick's closed expression to Daniel's glacial one. Not so much as a hint of goofiness in the vicinity.

Frederick nodded. 'Make sure you're back in time for the waltz.'

With that he moved away, through the throng of guests, and within moments had been absorbed into a group.

For a second Kaitlin stood, her high-heeled sandals rooted to the marquee floor, frozen by the surreal impossibility of Daniel's presence. Fear dried her mouth. How had he found her? What was he going to do? Questions crowded and jostled in her brain, even as she kept her expression neutral. Yet alongside the anxiety that stretched her nerves there was...*awareness*.

Try as she might, she couldn't stop the memories from tumbling back. Sensations, taste, passion, laughter...the feel of his touch skimming her skin... The very thought made her shiver across the nine-month gap.

Rein it in, Kaitlin.

Because clearly Daniel was not walking that path of memory—his expression displayed a cold anger that was *not* a happy omen for the forthcoming discussion.

Come on, Kaitlin.

It might still be all right—if he'd wanted to create a scene he surely would have done so by now.

'How about we take this outside?' he suggested, his voice hard.

Kaitlin shook her head. 'No. I don't want anyone to get the wrong idea about us.'

Lord knew she didn't want anyone to get *any* idea about them at all—even a glimmer of the truth had the potential to destroy her future.

He raised an eyebrow. 'Bit late to worry about that now, isn't it?'

'Shh! For goodness' sake, could you please keep your voice down? We need to be discreet.'

Her head spun, though she took pride in the knowledge that not a single observer would notice her inner turmoil. All that was on show was the poised, collected Lady Kaitlin Derwent, chatting politely to a wedding guest. Unless, of course, anyone actually overheard the content of the conversation…

He shook his head. 'Wrong. *You* need to be discreet. I couldn't care less. So, if you want discretion I suggest we take this outside. There's less chance we'll be overheard or interrupted out there.'

Daniel had a point, and surely there would be some guests outside. The afternoon sun shone down, and what could be more natural than she should show a guest the famed Derwent Manor gardens?

'OK. Fine.'

They walked towards the entrance of the marquee and somehow, from somewhere, Kaitlin summoned up conversation. 'So you're linked with the Caversham Foundation? That's inter-esting.'

Daniel's stride slowed as he stared at her, gen-uine incredulity etched on the craggy contours of his face. 'Are you for real? You want to make chit-chat?'

'For the benefit of the people watching us—yes, I do.'

'So your image matters that much to you?'

'Yes.' Her voice was flat. 'Haven't you heard? Image is everything.'

To her it truly was. The creation of Lady Kait-lin Derwent's image had been her own personal version of therapy—the way she'd coped after the kidnap fourteen years before. It had been her way to block out the memories, the fear that lived with her day and night, the coil of panic that lashed round her without warning. Being Lady Kaitlin allowed her to live her life.

'So, yes, seeing as we are supposed to be en-gaging in polite conversation, let's do that.'

He gave one last head-shake of disbelief. 'Sure. My association with the Caversham Foundation is actually the price your brother requested in return for a wedding invitation. On top of my donation to Derwent Manor—which was your father's stipulation.'

Keep walking.

'And you agreed to this just so you could talk to me?'

'Yes. It's a good cause, and an association with the Duke and Duchess of Fairfax and their son will be good publicity for my firm. Clients like things like that.'

'Which firm do you work for?'

'I'm CEO of Harrington Legal Services.'

Now her footsteps *did* falter. HLS was huge— a global law firm with offices in every major city in the world.

'In Barcelona you told me you were a lawyer.'

'I *am* a lawyer. And you aren't in any position to accuse *me* of messing with the truth.'

Touché.

Kaitlin quickened her pace slightly as they exited the marquee and stepped into the late-afternoon sunshine that bathed the lush green landscaped lawns with dappled light. Other guests stood in small groups as Kaitlin led the way along the gravelled path, lined with lush green manicured hedges, towards a bench she judged to be secluded, but not so isolated as to give anyone reason to gossip.

Once seated, she turned towards him, keeping her smile in place for the benefit of onlookers. 'So, why are you here, Daniel?'

CHAPTER THREE

IT WAS A good question. Why *was* he here? Sitting in the splendour of Derwent Manor's famed landscaped gardens. Nearby camellias provided vivid splashes of pink, and their bench overlooked the breathtaking glory of the rhododendron garden for which the Manor was famed.

But in truth the surroundings didn't matter; right now all that mattered was the woman next to him on the wooden bench in the sunshine. The woman he'd known as 'Lynette'. The woman whose true identity had turned out to be Lady Kaitlin Derwent.

Anger battled an unwanted stab of desire as he absorbed her sheer beauty.

Titian hair of a near-indescribable shade—tints of auburn interwoven with shades of reddish-gold—cascaded in loose waves to meet creamy bare shoulders that had his fingers tingling. Her dark green eyes met his gaze in a mixture of defiance, vulnerability and hope.

'Well?' she repeated. 'Why are you here?'

'Because I wanted to check for myself whether Lady Kaitlin Derwent and "Lynette" were one and the same.'

'How did you find out?'

'I saw a recent picture of you and Prince Frederick.'

Glaring up at him from the glossy cover of a celebrity magazine, the image had caught his eye at an airport lounge just weeks ago. About to look away something elusive had nagged at him: the set of Lady Kaitlin's head, the angle of her cheekbones...a willow-the-wisp of recognition.

'And you recognised me from that?'

'Not at first.'

At first he'd thought nothing of it. But some instinct had made him purchase his very first gossip rag and study the photograph further. One business flight later he'd known he must be losing the plot—big-time—but the conviction that Lady Kaitlin Derwent and his 'Lynette' were one and the same wouldn't quit. The more he'd researched Lady Kaitlin the more sure he'd become, preposterous though the idea was, that he'd found 'Lynette'.

'Until today I wasn't a hundred per cent sure.'

Her hands twisted together on her lap. Then, as if aware of the gesture, she loosed the grip. 'You could just have called me. This is a disaster—now you've made contact with my family...we have an association.' Horror etched her classical features. 'What if we end up meeting again?'

'Then so be it. I wanted to see you face to face—make sure beyond a shadow of a doubt that you are "Lynette". Without calling first and giving you a chance to lie. Again.'

Forcing himself to lean back, Daniel kept his anger in check.

'Plus, it's hard to call someone who didn't leave a number, didn't even give their real name, and who vanished without so much as a goodbye.'

'You knew it was one night only.'

A night of freedom.

'Yes, but I didn't know your "one night of freedom" was an aristocrat slumming it with the hoi-polloi.' Anger at her deception, wrath at his own stupidity in falling for her show, fuelled his words. 'Is that the new trend—to lose your vir—?'

Her poise broke and a laser of ire flashed in her eyes. 'Stop right there. How dare you? That is *not* what it was. That night was—'

Breaking off, she pressed her lips together and for a moment vulnerability lit those emerald-green eyes and momentarily sideswiped his anger.

'Was what?'

'It doesn't matter. I know it was shabby to leave like that, but I had no choice. In case you woke up and realised who I really was. Or someone might have recognised me...seen us together.'

Sheesh.

'Would that have been so bad?' Good thing his ego was in good shape.

'Yes.' The word was delivered with simplicity. 'The scandal would have been too much. Especially...'

'Especially because you were planning to marry a prince.'

'No! I mean... I hadn't decided what to do.' She twisted her hands into the teal-green folds of her skirt and then, as if realising what she was doing, she smoothed the material and pulled her shoulders back. 'I wasn't dating Frederick at the time, but I knew there was a possibility that I would in the future. I was a free agent that night, Daniel, and I didn't offer more than I could give. One night.'

'But you *lied*. And you took what I gave under false pretences. I wouldn't have spent the night with you in Barcelona if I'd known who you were and exactly what your gilded cage was.'

'Why not?' The question tumbled out and she pressed her lips together as if in regret.

'Because you were as good as promised to another man and I don't poach.' The idea was anathema—he'd watched his mother's repeated humiliation at his stepfather's numerous infidelities.

Kaitlin leant forward, shook her head, her red-gold hair swinging as if in emphasis. 'I was *not* promised to anyone. Frederick and I had no understanding at that point. It was simply an idea that my parents had put to me. He hadn't approached me—there had been no discussions.'

'But you *knew*.' His voice was implacable. 'All the time you were with me you knew that you would soon be dating someone else. You as good as said it.'

'One night of freedom before I step into a gilded cage.'

Her words in Barcelona had been poignant. Because he knew all too well the iron bars of a gilded cage.

He'd grown up in one—benefited from the gilding, the luxuries, the power, the money, the lifestyle. At what point had he suspected that all those advantages had been bought with money raised from illegal sources? When had he realised what his mother had done?

Guilt coated his insides. She'd done it for him—to give him all those advantages. His father had been dead, she had been destitute, and so his mother had stepped into a gilded cage, married into the mob, and taken two-year-old Daniel in with her.

Enough. That part of his life was over. Here and now he focused on Kaitlin, studied her cool, aloof expression, and felt curiosity as to her motivations surface. 'I don't get why you took such an enormous risk.'

Because every scrap of research he had done

on Kaitlin Derwent had shown that risk wasn't in her personality. Never a hair out of place... always ready with a witty quip or the correct comment. Always serene, poised, calm and in control—not the type of person to risk a scandal for a one-night stand. Yet that was exactly what she had done.

'It doesn't matter.' Her tone had lost all colour, and a sudden image of 'Lynette' filled his mind—her vivacity, the way she'd laughed, spoken, enthused. It seemed almost impossible that Lynette and Kaitlin were one and the same.

Not his business. Kaitlin was right. It didn't matter—he'd come here to satisfy his curiosity, confirm his near conviction. No more.

Kaitlin glanced around. 'We've been out here too long; people will start to talk soon. I need to go. This is Gabe's wedding—I don't want to ruin it in any way.' She closed her eyes for a second. 'But we need to finish this conversation.'

They did? As far as he was concerned it was over bar the farewell. But Kaitlin clearly disagreed.

'I'd appreciate a few more minutes of your time. Maybe tomorrow?'

'Sure.' Curiosity prompted his acquiescence. Along with the knowledge that it was never wise to refuse information. All good lawyers knew that information was power. The last thing he wanted was for this farce to come back and bite him in the future. If Lady Kaitlin Derwent believed there was an issue to discuss then he'd go along for the ride.

'Breakfast. Tomorrow. Faircliffe Hotel. I'll book a private room.'

'Thank you.' She gave a fatalistic lift of her shoulders. 'I'll be there.'

The morning spring sunshine slanted through the windows of the hotel bedroom, reflecting off the mirror where Kaitlin surveyed her reflection. She put the final touches to her discreet layer of make-up—the mask that ensured Lady Kaitlin retained her image of cool perfection.

'I wish you'd tell me what is going on,' her sister said from where she sat on the bed.

Not surprisingly, given it was the closest hotel in the neighbourhood, Cora and her husband, Rafael, had stayed in the same hotel as Daniel the previous night. Kaitlin had figured it was better to tell Cora about the meeting rather than have her twin waylay her en route to breakfast. Now she was beginning to think she should just have kept quiet. Cora had insisted on seeing Kaitlin before the meeting, and her dark blue eyes reflected her usual intuitive discern.

Kaitlin met her sister's gaze in the mirror. 'Nothing is going on.'

'Rubbish. I'm your twin, Kait. There are times when I just *know*, and this is one of them.'

It was true—there was a bond, despite how different she and Cora were. Years before, when the kidnap had occurred, her twin had been distraught, refusing to believe her parents assertion that Kaitlin was staying with friends.

There were times when Kaitlin wished she had rebelled against her parents' dictate and confided in Cora. But she hadn't—she'd convinced herself that if she supressed the memories, locked them away, they would become a dream, lose the sharp edges of reality. So she'd done what her parents had instructed her to do—and never told a soul what had happened.

'What's done is done, Kaitlin. The important thing now is to forget it ever happened. And

never, ever disobey us again.' The Duchess's stern voice had hardened further. *'You understand that no one must ever know. It shows us as weak and, worse, those kidnappers have photos of you that cannot be made public. You will not disgrace the Derwent name.'*

'Kait?' Cora's voice was edged with concern, and Kaitlin focused on her twin. 'Is it something to do with the Prince? Because I've wanted to talk to you about Frederick for a long time and...'

Kaitlin had used guile and every conversational trick in the library to avoid the subject. 'I don't need to discuss Fredrick.'

'Well, I do. All I want to say is that before I met Rafael I would have done anything to win Mum and Dad's approval. Because I thought that was the way to win their love.'

'I—'

Cora raised a hand. 'Let me finish. I *need* to say this. Don't marry him if you don't love him. Love has transformed my life and I'd like you to have an opportunity to feel the way I feel.'

And there was the crux of the matter. Lady Kaitlin didn't do feelings—*couldn't* feel, didn't want to experience the tsunami of emotions that might be unleashed if she allowed feelings in.

'Cora, I am truly happy for you, and your happiness, but everyone experiences happiness in a different way. My road is different from yours.' Ignoring the small sigh from her sister, she glanced at her watch. 'Now, I've got to go.'

Suspicion narrowed Cora's blue eyes. 'That's another thing. I'm getting a vibe about Daniel Harrington as well. Remind me why you're meeting him.'

'I told you. He wants to discuss a project— and, given the amount he donated to the Derwent Manor restoration fund, I think it's polite to at least see what he has to say. *And* he's linked to the Caversham Foundation.'

That should reassure Cora, bearing in mind her friendship with Ethan and Ruby Caversham.

Kaitlin rose from the dressing table in one graceful move and cast a last look in the mirror, taking comfort in the fact that outwardly no one except her pesky twin would be able to tell her inner self was in turmoil. The dove-grey light wool coat dress was perfect for the occasion. It spoke of an aloof elegance with businesslike overtones that would assure any nosey reporter that this breakfast had no innuendo attached. The intricate hand-stitched ribbon embroidered around the neck and falling across the front gave it the Kaitlin Derwent 'edge', and she gave a small satisfied nod.

'I'll see you later, Cora. And quit worrying.'

As Kaitlin exited the room and made her way down the carpeted grand staircase of the country hotel her heart pounded her ribcage. It was only the years of practice that kept her upright. Her gaze darted around the lobby in an automatic check for danger even as she focused on keeping her gait unhurried.

She managed a smile for Sophia, the member of staff who manned the small desk that led to the breakfast room. 'I have a meeting with Daniel Harrington.'

The girl nodded with enthusiasm. 'Mr Harrington has booked for a private room. Come through here.'

'Thank you.' She followed the girl into a small room and braced herself as Daniel rose from the table to greet her.

'Lady Kaitlin.'

To her relief his voice was formal, but as she met his gaze she saw something flash in his eyes and her own body instinctively responded. Knowing her voice would suffer from lack of breath, she nodded in acknowledgement.

'Can I get you anything?' Sophia asked,

'We're good, thanks.'

There was silence when the young woman had left.

Get it together, Kaitlin.

If only this man didn't affect her so much. Her expert eye recognised the quality of the understated light blue silk cotton shirt and suit trousers. But it wasn't the expensive clothes—it was the raw energy they contained, the solid, muscular bulk of his body, the strength of his craggy features, the square determination of his jaw and the set of his lips.

Lips that had given her such aching pleasure she nearly shivered with the memory.

Get it together now, *Kaitlin.*

He gestured to the side table pushed against the wall of the room. 'Help yourself to food.'

Kaitlin contemplated refusing, unsure whether she could physically eat, given the fact her tummy was busy tying itself up in a lanyard of knots. But this was supposedly a business breakfast, and therefore she'd do better to play along. The last thing she wanted was for the hotel staff to notice anything amiss.

Two minutes later she seated herself at the circular table, with a plate holding a croissant, a dab of butter and a small pot of strawberry jam in front of her. Somehow she had to focus—she was here to negotiate herself out of this mess. Channelling every single iota of her inner poise, she managed a cool smile. Whatever it cost her she would not show Daniel even a particle of her discomfort.

'So, Kaitlin. You requested this meeting. Why?'

'I need to know what you plan to do.'

For a fleeting second confusion flashed across his face, and then a small mirthless smile tipped his lips up. 'You're worried I'll go public with the whole Barcelona story?'

'Yes.'

In truth, the idea of the press getting hold of this made her quake. Her parents would… Her imagination couldn't even begin to conjure up the Duke's and Duchess's reactions. But it was more than that…

'I realise you have no obligation not to,' she continued quietly, 'but it wouldn't just impact me. The scandal would affect Prince Frederick as well.'

The House of Lycander had been besmirched by more than its fair share of disgrace and rocked by tragedy, and the idea that she might add to Frederick's troubles filled her with horror.

'I don't want my stupidity to discredit Frederick or make him look a fool in the eyes of the media.'

'Because you love him?'

The question was posed as though the answer mattered and it caused her vocal chords to tighten.

'Or because it would make your relationship and marriage to him problematical?'

Perhaps she should lie—claim that she *did* love Frederick, throw herself on Daniel's mercy. *Ha!* Instinct informed her that that wouldn't work, because she sensed he didn't have any. But, more than that, she didn't want to lie—she'd lied enough.

'That's none of your business. I will not discuss Prince Frederick with you. That's not fair to him.'

'You didn't worry about fairness in Barcelona.'

'I told you—I hadn't met him then. Or at least I hadn't started to date him.'

'But you knew you were going to.'

Daniel's voice was soft, but the edge could have cut a diamond. Easy to imagine him in a courtroom now.

'All the time you were with me you knew that you would soon be dating someone else.'

The contempt in his voice made her feel exposed and she leant forward, needing him to understand even as she knew she shouldn't care about his opinion.

'Yes.' There could be no denial there, but she'd be damned if she apologised either. 'But I didn't plan that night. I didn't go to Barcelona to have a one-night stand.'

'Why *did* you go?'

'I had a moment of panic.'

'No. A moment of panic is when you have a few drinks, breathe into a paper bag or eat your bodyweight in chocolate. It's not when you assume a fake identity and sleep with a stranger.'

'OK. So I had a *spectacular* moment of panic.'

'Because of Prince Frederick? That seems extreme. No one was going to march you to the altar on the spot.'

'I know that.'

How to explain panic to this man? A man who clearly knew who he was and what he wanted from life. To Kaitlin, panic was a mortal enemy—kept on a leash, tamed by her determination not to let it conquer her. Time had taught her the best way to achieve dominance was control—if she micromanaged every second of her life, created a secure zone, a persona that was in command, that way she won.

'I just wanted some space to process the future...some time out. The plan was to stay in my hotel room and order room service. Instead...' She tipped a palm up and let out a sigh.

Instead she'd deviated from the script for the first time in a decade, stepped out of her comfort zone and into disaster.

'Instead you ended up with me. It doesn't make sense. As far as I can tell, from the publicity that surrounds you, you are the personification of discretion. You've never so much as been caught tipsy, and any relationships you have had haven't caused even a breath of scandal. As for you and Prince Frederick—you haven't even been seen holding hands in public...'

Impossible to explain that there was no spark between her and Prince Frederick—had never been a spark with any man until Daniel. Dating Frederick was calm, correct and dutiful. In truth that had surprised her as much as it had relieved her. Prince Frederick of Lycander had once been a noted playboy—had 'dated', for want of a better euphemism, plenty of women, and been photographed on yachts and in night clubs. But clearly that wasn't the way he treated a possible wife. Formal duty characterised their relationship, and that suited her fine.

'I agree it didn't make sense. I acted out of character and it was a mistake.' Of enormous proportions.

The sparks between her and Daniel had set off an inferno that could affect the rest of her life.

'So now you've decided to enter the gilded

cage? That's the gilded cage you were talking about in Barcelona, isn't it?'

The words slammed into her—seemed to echo across the months.

'The Lycander marriage.'

Kaitlin summoned as much aristocratic hauteur as was possible. 'My marriage is my business and I know what I'm doing.'

Amazing she could say that with a straight face. No! She *did* know what she was doing; it was just this man, this horrible scenario, that was messing with her head.

'There is nothing wrong with a gilded cage.'

'Dammit. There is *everything* wrong with a gilded cage.'

The force in his voice made her jump, caused her heart to pound.

'It's a prison of the worst kind.'

Bleakness flashed across his blue eyes and for a mad second she wanted to reach out and offer comfort. *Ridiculous.* She had to focus on what was important here.

'You are entitled to your opinion, but I disagree.'

His fingers drummed the snowy white linen

of the tablecloth and his gaze seemed to bore into her soul. 'That's not what you thought nine months ago.'

'Yes, it is. I had a moment of insanity that night, but however mad I was I always knew what my future held.'

Daniel shook his head and she wondered why this mattered so much to him. She felt an urge to ask—a wish that this conversation didn't have to be so antagonistic. A sudden memory of the conversations they'd shared that Barcelona night clouded her mind: the ease, the banter, the sharing of opinions. Compared with the sophisticated, carefully constructed exchange of her talk with Frederick. *Enough.* Bad enough that her body was on alert—heaven help her if her mind joined the party.

'And I should never have jeopardised it with a meaningless one-night stand.'

His eyebrows rose. 'Meaningless?' he repeated softly.

'Meaningless on any real level.' It was impossible to infuse her words with more than a mocking semblance of truth—not when she knew that their night together had been little short of a miracle for her.

'You sure about that?'

His voice deepened and Kaitlin caught her breath on the smallest of gasps. She dropped her gaze from the look in his eye. The ice-blue had darkened to cobalt and she knew what she would see in their depths—the memory of the levels, the sheer *heights* of the passion they had scaled. Heat crept up her cheekbones and her gaze lingered on his hands, on their strength, their capability, and an image flashed into her brain. The touch of his fingers as they'd caressed her skin…her own fingers trailing down the skin of his bare back…the ripple of muscle, the taste of…

Momentarily she closed her eyes, made dizzy by a mix of horror and sheer sensuous memory. *Enough.* That had been a night of madness, and if anything it had shown her that spontaneity led to disaster. Reinforced her need to be Lady Kaitlin Derwent—poised, calm, serene and safe. *That* was who she needed to be now; being 'Lynette' had landed her in a mess of horrific proportions, and right now she needed to stay focused on getting herself out.

She could only hope that the effort it took to keep her voice steady wasn't beading her brow with perspiration.

Kaitlin looked down at the croissant on her plate…realised that at some point in this quagmire of a conversation she had crumbled the flaky pastry into a pile of crumbs. It was not her usual behaviour, and impatience rippled through her along with a touch of panic. She could not afford to unravel now.

'Meaningless,' she repeated, and this time she succeeded in imbuing her voice with aloofness. 'Surely you aren't claiming it meant anything to *you*?'

If she'd hoped to gain his agreement she was disappointed.

'Of course it did. Not because I wanted more, but because I liked and respected "Lynette" and I hoped that the night was meaningful to us both.'

Ouch.

The words hurt, but she knew she deserved them. It had been poor form to deceive him and it had been disingenuous of her to say that the night had been meaningless. But she wouldn't—*couldn't*—back down now. Daniel Harrington had the power to bring her name and, more importantly, the name of Lycander into disrepute.

'None of this is relevant, Mr Harrington. I need to know whether you plan to go public.'

Her breath caught in her lungs as she waited for his answer.

There was a silence as he looked at her, and then he shook his head. 'Is that all you care about?'

'Right now, yes. And I won't apologise for that. This isn't only my name at stake—it's Frederick's as well.'

His lips twisted in a grimace. 'To say nothing of mine. So you have no need to fret, Kaitlin. I won't go public. Believe it or not, I have no wish to be embroiled in some sordid media scandal.'

The intensity of his voice alerted her, and she couldn't help but wonder at the nuance of revulsion. As if he sensed her interest he shrugged. 'I'm a lawyer—a serious one—it wouldn't be good for my business.'

That made sense, and yet she had an instinct that there was more to it than that. Not that it mattered—the point was that he would keep their time in Barcelona to himself. But even as relief washed over her, her doubts grew. Could Daniel *really* not want anything? Could she trust him?

Even though an irrational gut feeling told her she could, she *knew* the world didn't turn like that. A woman she'd trusted completely had been the one to collude with her kidnappers. Since then she'd made a point of not listening to her instincts—after all, she was living proof of how foolish trust could be.

'So, you'll walk away?'

There was a second's hesitation as he studied her, and she swore she could see a flicker of concern in his ice-blue eyes.

'Yes. But I'll give you the same advice that I gave "Lynette" nine months ago. Don't enter a gilded cage unless you have the means to leave.'

'OK.' Once again she wondered why it mattered so much to him. 'And, thank you, Daniel.'

He rose to his feet and held out a hand. 'Good luck, Kaitlin.'

Rising to her feet, she looked at his hand for a fraction too long, absurdly worried about so much as a touch. *Truly absurd.* She pulled on a smile that hopefully combined farewell with gratitude and placed her hand in his.

Not so absurd after all. His touch made her feel… It didn't matter what it made her feel. Because it shouldn't make her feel *anything.*

'Goodbye, Daniel.'

As she turned to exit the room she waited for relief to wash over her. But instead her tummy felt weighted with a ridiculous sense of loss. An echo of nine months before, when she had walked away from that hotel room in Barcelona.

CHAPTER FOUR

Two weeks later

KAITLIN STARED IN the mirror, marvelled at the serenity of her reflection that thankfully showed no indication of the inner hysterics gallivanting inside her. But she shouldn't be surprised. After all this was her forte—looking the part.

Her outfit was the perfect choice for a woman about to receive a marriage proposal from a prince. The flared cream trouser suit was cool and casual, and saved from blandness by the sparkly shimmer of a silver-grey camisole-style blouse. Her freshly washed hair fell in simple loose waves to her shoulders, and her make-up epitomised the art of discretion.

Time to go—even though her nerves quivered as she exited her old bedroom in Derwent Manor, taking comfort from the familiar smooth sheen of the oak under her fingertips as she descended the stairs and walked past the line of portraits of her ancestors. It was easy to imagine them all applauding with approval at the prospective alliance.

As she entered the lounge Prince Frederick turned from where he stood at the ornate fireplace.

'Kaitlin.'

'Frederick.'

He stepped towards her, his face expressionless, a picture of formal decorum, dressed in a tailor-made suit, his hazel eyes unreadable, but without a hint of warmth.

This is not how it is supposed to be, pointed out a small, insistent voice at the back of her brain.

And as if he too realised that, Frederick smiled.

But the smile didn't reach his eyes and Kaitlin, a connoisseur of smiles, recognised its stoic element. He took another step forward, so he was near enough to take her hand, though of course he didn't.

'Thank you for seeing me. I assume you know why we are here?'

'Yes.'

Don't enter a gilded cage unless you have the means to leave.

Daniel's words rang in her brain. *Stupid.* A man she barely knew. Yet a man she had trusted with not only her own name but that of the House of Lycander. A house that had been plagued with scandal enough to rock the throne with sufficient force to require the Prince to seek a marriage that would prove to his people that their sovereign cared. For that Prince Frederick needed a bride untainted by even the smallest germ of scandal.

Realisation weighted her tummy—she'd had no right to place her blind trust in a veritable stranger…to gamble with Prince Frederick's name without his knowledge.

'Wait.' Kaitlin raised a hand. 'There is something I need to tell you.'

Dread tightened her chest as she braced herself for the storm about to break.

'What the…?' Daniel stared down at the headline that confronted him from the top of his newly cleared desk.

'I thought you might be interested,' his PA explained, her voice carefully devoid of emotion. 'As you attended the Earl's wedding and...'

Daniel wrenched his gaze away from the laptop screen that displayed a website devoted to celebrity gossip and eyed Caroline, who returned his gaze expressionlessly.

Caroline Winterbourne looked as cool, collected and indifferent as ever, but Daniel knew differently. He'd given her a chance, despite her prison record, and in return she offered unassailable loyalty.

'I'll leave you to it.'

Daniel returned his attention to the article and an expletive dropped from his lips as the words slammed into his retinas.

Lycander Split: It's All Off!
Lady Kaitlin Derwent and Prince Frederick of Lycander have announced the end of their relationship after 'mutual agreement'. Neither side is willing to elaborate, but friends and acquaintances have declared shock and surprise.

The couple have been seen together for months and the world had awaited the an-

*nouncement of an engagement—not a break-
up. However, the ex-couple insist they will
remain friends.*

*Watch this space as we try to discover the
real reason behind the surprise split...*

His intercom buzzed. 'Daniel, I have an April
Fotherington on the line. She's a celebrity reporter. Shall I get rid of her?'

Caroline's tone suggested she'd be happy to
bury the body as well.

'No. I'll talk to her.' There was a click and then
he said, 'Daniel Harrington speaking.'

'Mr Harrington. Thank you for speaking with
me. I wanted to get your reaction to the break-
up between Lady Kaitlin Derwent and Prince
Frederick.'

'I don't *have* a reaction. Am I supposed to?'

'My sources inform me that you and Lady
Kaitlin were spotted deep in private conversation at the Earl of Wycliffe's wedding recently.'

'That is hardly a basis for me to have formed
any opinion on Lady Kaitlin's relationship with
Prince Frederick.'

'Hmm...' The reporter's tone was heavy with

scepticism. 'Thank you for your time. Maybe we'll speak again soon.'

Daniel put down the phone and cursed under his breath. He drummed his fingers on the desk and then picked up the phone. 'Caroline, please can you get me Lady Kaitlin Derwent's number?'

'Leave it with me.'

Twenty minutes later he was en route across London. Forty minutes later he had parked in the vicinity of Lady Kaitlin's Chelsea flat and alighted from the car. He eyed the group of reporters that crowded the pavement outside.

Walk as if you have the right and then you do have the right.

Advice given to him by his stepbrother— the man he'd once revered more than any other being.

Moving through the baying throng of press, he ignored all the shouted questions, reached the door and banged on its navy blue surface in the pre-agreed code. Kaitlin pulled the door open a crack and he squeezed through.

Even now, when circumstance dictated frustration and anger, her beauty socked him. Her stance, her poise, the strength of her features, the vividness of her eyes—all endowed her with looks that wouldn't fade with the ravages of time.

He followed her into a lounge that exuded elegance and good taste, where she turned to face him. 'You said on the phone that we may have a problem.'

'April Fotherington rang me an hour ago for my reaction to your split with Prince Frederick. She suspects I am involved and I believe she will dig until she uncovers a link between us.'

The clenching of her hands was an indication that the news was less than welcome.

'That woman has got some sort of super-sense about me. Probably because she has made it her business to be the Derwent family media expert.'

'Well, she will not become an expert on *me* because I have no intention of being pulled into some media gossip frenzy.'

'You may have no choice.' Emerald eyes lasered bitterness at him. 'Why, Daniel? Why did you have to come to the wedding? Why did you track me down? Come to that, why did I ever agree to have a drink with you?' She gave a shake of her head and took a deep breath. 'Doesn't matter. You can't turn the clock back.'

Her voice echoed motes of sadness across the air and he knew with gut deep certainty that she wasn't just referring to her present predicament. *Not his business.*

'No you can't. Time cannot be dialled back. That is why it's always best to face forward.' That was the vow he'd made when he'd walked away from his family, from his life of wealth and privilege.

Kaitlin sank down onto the sofa. 'Unfortunately what I am facing is a tabloid tsunami that you have only made worse. Once April discovers you hot-footed it over here I am doomed— she'll have all the "evidence" she needs to know there is a juicy story to unearth.'

'So that still bothers you?'

'Of course it does. If April digs up Barcelona I am the one who'll bear the brunt of the damage. My image would be in tatters. I'd be painted as the woman who cheated on the Prince of Lycander and I have no wish to embroil myself in that kind of mire. In addition, this isn't Prince

Frederick's fault—it is mine, and I feel I owe it to him to avert the scandal if I can.'

Her words rang true, yet for a second her gaze fluttered away and the slightest rose tint flushed the high angle of her cheekbone.

Irrelevant—his only concern here was to scotch the scandal. For his own sake.

'OK. Then we are on the same page. I came here because I have a plan.'

Wary surprise touched her expression. 'The only possible plan is to deny any connection between us.'

Daniel shook his head. 'Too late for that. April will find out we met for breakfast and she'll keep on digging. I propose to head her off at the pass. But to do that I need information—the real reason you and the Prince split.'

Her gaze dropped, but not before he saw a glint of hurt in her eyes—a glimmer she erased before she raised her head.

'That is not your concern.'

'Yes, it is. If we want to avoid a scandal then we need to put all our cards on the table.'

A half-laugh totally devoid of mirth fell from her lips. 'By that you mean *I* need to put my cards on the table, when I don't even understand why this matters so much to *you*.'

'I told you. I have an international reputation to maintain as well, and I have no wish to see my name splashed across the tabloids. It would hardly make me look good in court.'

Though that would be the least of his worries if his connection to the mob was revealed. The adverse effect of that would reverberate through his company and impact on his employees, and he would not let that happen.

Her slim shoulders lifted in a shrug. 'I'm not an idiot either, and I'm pretty sure that's not your full hand of cards.'

'That is irrelevant. What matters now is that we prevent April Fotherington from unearthing what happened in Barcelona.'

A memory of that night, the sheer magic of their connection, sneaked up from nowhere and blindsided him with a bombardment of images. He rubbed a hand over his face, swiped them away. Their physical connection had been based on illusion, and as such its worth was *zero*. In any currency.

'To do that I need to know why you and the Prince broke up.'

'Give me a minute.'

For the first time since he'd entered Daniel looked round the room. It was impeccably furnished, and good taste abounded—neutral cream walls a backdrop for a fourth wall of elegant patterned wallpaper with a splash of colour in the bird-themed print. Pictures dotted the walls in a mix of modern and retro, and the simply striped upholstered furniture looked both comfortable and stylish.

Yet something grated on his nerves; it was the knowledge that the lounge looked exactly as Lady Kaitlin's lounge *should* look—ready for a photographer to descend at any moment. The fact that there wasn't so much as a hint of 'Lynette' to be seen.

Kaitlin gestured to the armchair opposite. 'OK. I'll bite. The Prince and I split up because I told him about Barcelona.'

Daniel stared at her, wondered if perhaps his ears had ceased to function, whether his brain had somehow rewritten the signals and garbled her words. 'You *told* Prince Frederick about Barcelona. Why?'

'It wasn't fair to put his good name at stake without his knowledge. I couldn't place trust in your discretion on Frederick's behalf—he needed to make that decision for himself.'

A mix of emotion hit him—chagrin at her lack of faith, and admiration and surprise at a level of principle he hadn't expected from the woman who had duped him…a woman set on a marriage made of glitter and lined with gold.

'So he decided to break up with you because of the potential scandal or because he felt angry at the thought of you with another man?'

Weariness made her shoulders slump for a fraction of a heartbeat and then she straightened, dropped her hands to her lap from their mid-rise to a defensive fold.

'The former. Frederick needs a scandal-free bride and I no longer qualify.'

'In which case I could talk to him and convince him I won't go public.'

'It wouldn't work; his view is that it happened, therefore there is always a risk of dis-

covery. However small the risk, he doesn't feel it's worth it.'

Didn't feel *Kaitlin* was worth it. That had to hurt. Whatever the ins and outs of their relationship, however political or convenient it had been, they had spent nine months together.

'And they say chivalry is dead.'

'I don't want chivalry—I messed up and there are consequences.' A shadow flitted across the emerald-green eyes—one that spoke of weariness and a bitter knowledge of how cause and effect worked. 'Anyway, I've given you the information you requested, so now it's your turn. Tell me your plan to deal with April Fotherington.'

The idea that had spun into his mind as he'd travelled across London coalesced into a tangible reality. 'OK. Listen up.'

CHAPTER FIVE

A PLAN—A POTENTIAL solution to their predicament was a good thing, right? Kaitlin tried to focus, to think... But right now it was hard to think at all through the confusion brought on by Daniel's unexpected arrival on the scene. A veritable knight in shining armour. *Not.*

Daniel's involvement suited his own purposes—her rescue was a mere by-product, and she'd do well to install that fact in her memory banks. But no matter—the past twenty-four hours had been abysmal, as she'd watched her future spiral out of her control, so if she could ride his coattails out of this mess then she would.

'Go ahead.'

He rose to his feet in a lithe ripple of muscle. Clad in blue jeans and a dark blue T-shirt, he exuded energy as he paced the beige coir carpet.

'At the wedding I said I had a project to discuss with you. We'll run with that story. As

I told you, in return for an invitation to your brother's wedding I agreed to make a donation to the Caversham Foundation. Gabriel insisted that the donation not be monetary—instead he demanded I pledge a week of my time. I spoke with Ethan Caversham and I agreed.'

'Why?' The question was not germane to the situation, but curiosity propelled the question from her lips.

'I wanted the invitation—your brother and Ethan are valuable contacts—and Ethan is a very persuasive man. Enough that I agreed to take this week off work. I'm to travel to the Highlands, where I will spend three days participating in outdoor activities with a group of troubled teenagers. Then I fly to Venice to host a fundraising ball.' He halted and turned to face her. 'I propose that *you* come with me. What do you think?'

Say what?

He stood there as if he had come up with the equivalent of a winning lottery ticket instead of the nuttiest scheme ever.

'I don't think anything. I *know* you've run mad.'

'That is because you haven't thought it through.'

'Nope. It's because it doesn't make any sense—we would need to spend a whole week together.' The idea fuzzed her brain with cotton wool even as her insides twisted in panic. 'That will only fuel speculation about us—not prevent it.'

'Not if we play it right. The story provides a perfectly logical explanation for the time we've spent together, both at the wedding and at breakfast the next day. I tried to persuade you to get involved—you couldn't because of your commitments with Prince Frederick. So when I heard about the split I hot-footed it over here to see if I could convince you to join me now.'

There was a certain plausibility about it, but... 'That might work as a cover, but I could have still refused to join you. There is no need for me to actually *come* to Scotland or Venice.' The idea shortened her breath, pierced her chest with the stab of anxiety that preceded panic.

Chill, Kaitlin.

'But it would be better if you did come.'

'Better for whom?'

'Better for the project. Right now the press is

focused on you—you could make a real difference…raise awareness of the Caversham Foundation by a substantial amount.' His eyebrows
rose with more than a hint of derision. 'Think
of your image as well. A refusal to participate
wouldn't look good.'

Whereas an agreement would be an opportunity to remodel Lady Kaitlin—transition her
from prospective royal bride to a woman who
had moved on from her break-up in a positive
manner, the champion of a good cause that she
genuinely believed in.

Yet caution still raised its head. 'The press will
try to find a romantic angle.'

'Let them try. They won't be able to locate it,
because it doesn't exist.' His mouth twisted in
a wry upturn that held more than a hint of challenge. 'Unless, of course, you're worried you'll
succumb to my deadly charm?'

Kaitlin narrowed her eyes. 'In your dreams,
Daniel.' Been there, got the T-shirt and never
again.

'Then what are you so worried about? Worst-
case scenario is that they speculate—you're
a free agent now.' He eyed her for a moment,

fingers drumming on his thigh, and then he snapped his fingers. 'Unless you are hoping for a reconciliation with Prince Frederick?' Disdain dripped from his voice. 'Is that the plan—did he agree that if you weather the storm you will requalify as a Lycander bride?'

'No!' His contempt stung. 'There is no plan. But it's...complicated.'

With an effort she kept the crack of emotion from her voice as scenes from the previous day filled her mind.

The Duke and Duchess had taken disappoint-ment to new heights—their frustration had filled the living room at Derwent Manor with palpable waves of fury.

'You have let us down, Kaitlin. Not just us, but the Derwent name. The only way to redeem yourself is to get him back. Your destiny is with the House of Lycander—we want at least one grandchild with royal blood in his veins. Is that understood?'

The message had been loud and clear, and had been followed by the outline of a 'Win Frederick Back' action plan that had made her burn with humiliation. Yet she had listened in silence—had neither agreed to obey nor expressed refusal to comply. It had seemed the easiest option until she figured out for herself what she wanted to do. For months she'd been on a path and now... now she felt as though the proverbial rug had been pulled from under her designer wedge shoes.

'So, explain.'

The blue of his eyes held not so much as a glint of compassion, but at least his censure had been put on hold.

'This marriage is important to my parents and they believe I should keep my options open. I don't want to rock the boat.'

'You can't marry Prince Frederick for your parents' sake. They have no right to ask that of you.'

The sheer intensity of his voice rocked her backwards. 'They have every right to ask. My father is recovering from a heart attack and my brother and sister have both made marriages my parents' disapprove of. I have it within my power to make them happy by marrying a wealthy, handsome prince. It seemed like a no brainer.'

'*Seemed,*' he repeated. 'Past tense. What about

now?' He tipped his palms up in patent disbelief. 'The wealthy, handsome Prince has ruthlessly discarded you for fear of scandal. You can't possibly still want to marry him.'

Kaitlin resisted the urge to cover her ears and tune out his questions. She had erected a block against Prince Frederick's judgement. But now his words buzzed through the barrier like pellets of venom.

'I am sorry, Kaitlin—you would have made a good Lycander princess, but I can't take the risk of scandal or ridicule. Not now. My bride needs to be untainted by even a breath of scandal. You no longer qualify.'

For a moment the meaning of his words hadn't dawned on her—and then the realisation that nine months could be dismissed so summarily had had her reeling, caused a wire of irrational hurt and anger to tighten her chest. Clearly once again she wasn't worth fighting for; the threat of scandal outweighed her value as a person.

All those years ago her parents had made it plain that they wouldn't expose her kidnappers— wouldn't bring them to justice because of the potential smearing of the Derwent name. Now history had repeated itself with a vengeance.

It didn't matter—she wouldn't let it matter. Lady Kaitlin Derwent did *not* succumb to feelings. She had learnt to lock them down. Thus she had rid herself of pain, anxiety and the slither of horrific memories. So no way would she be goaded into emotion now.

Rising from the sofa, she faced him. 'My association with Prince Frederick was an alliance, not a relationship, and as such he had the right to break it if expedient. End of.'

'But you want to keep your options open to renew that alliance?'

His expression had dialled right back to disdain, but this time she steeled herself to suck it up. This conversation had gone far enough—exceeded the parameters of her comfort zone by a long way.

'It's always wise to keep your options open. Let's go back to your plan.'

'Your call. You're the one with the concerns about the possibility of a romantic angle.'

Instinct warned her that a week with Daniel

Harrington might lead to disaster, but logic re-
iterated the benefits.

'I'm in.'

'Good. Let's face the press on your doorstep
now. After that, I'm flying out to Scotland early
tomorrow—we might as well travel together.'

'No! Wait!' Seeing the surprise in his eyes,
she dialled down the volume of her response. 'I
mean, yes, but I need more information before
we leave.'

New places had the ability to overwhelm her
and trigger a panic attack, so she needed information so that she could prepare, research, lay
the groundwork to minimise the chance. Plus she
had to ensure she had knowledge of the correct
image Lady Kaitlin should project, which facet
of her persona would be on show.

'So would it be possible to brief me more thoroughly after we do the press interview?'

'No problem—we can combine it with dinner.'

'Great.' Her tummy was as hollow as the adjective—after all the last time she'd had dinner
with Daniel Harrington...

Stop. Don't go there.

* * *

Daniel glanced sideways at Kaitlin as they traversed the busy London streets en route to a restaurant of her choosing. Her elusive rose scent tantalised him, brought back unwanted reminders of another city, another time.

Another woman.

Once again he marvelled at the difference between 'Lynette' and Kaitlin, squashed the urge to see if he could delve beneath the layers of Kaitlin to free 'Lynette'.

Get a grip.

That perfume had clearly sent him towards delirium. No one needed freeing. From anywhere.

'It's here.' Kaitlin slowed down and gestured to a small restaurant. 'Cora and I eat here sometimes. It's private, but it won't give the wrong idea.'

As they entered Daniel saw what she meant. The effect was both quirky and fun; the mezzanine deck of the restaurant, where a number of booths were located, was approached by ladders, and the clientele was a mix of parents out with their kids, groups of friends and the occasional couple.

'Lady Kaitlin.' A stocky dark-haired man came forward. 'Welcome. Will there be reporters who need to be quietly ejected?'

'Hi, Carlos. We should be safe today.'

Daniel hoped so—the press had decamped from her door, having seemed to swallow their story, delivered with admirable aplomb by Kaitlin. It was a dexterity he had only been able to admire: the way she had sidestepped personal questions, explained her enthusiasm for the opportunity to support a cause her siblings already espoused. Though whether April Fotherington would fall for it or not was yet to be seen.

'Then follow me.'

They climbed to the upper level, where Carlos ushered them into a wooden booth hung with low lighting that gave a homely impression of warmth, enhanced by the warm polish of the rustic pine table between high-backed benches, padded with lengths of cheerful red cushion.

'I recommend the special.'

'I'm good with that,' Kaitlin said.

'That's fine with me too,' Daniel concurred.

'Then leave it all to me.' With a beaming smile Carlos departed.

'I hope that's all right? The food is good, it's not pretentious, and whilst Carlos isn't averse to a little publicity he draws the line if it becomes too intrusive.'

'Did you bring Prince Frederick here?' Lord knew where *that* had come from—it hardly mattered.

'No.' Her hand rose to tuck a tendril of hair behind her ear, and then she reached down into her bag and pulled out a notebook and pen. 'Give me five minutes, please, to list some questions, and then we can start.'

He watched as she bent over the notebook and started to write, took in the classical slant of her features, the glory of her hair, tinted with flecks of red and gold by the light, her small intent frown, the graceful line of her neck. Once again desire tugged at his gut, and it was a relief when a waiter appeared with sparkling wine and a bowl of glistening green and black olives.

And still she continued to write—until his limited store of patience ran out and he cleared his throat with theatrical emphasis.

Kaitlin looked up and her lips twisted in a

small guilty moue. 'Sorry. I got a bit absorbed. Let's get started.'

Daniel pushed the olives towards her. 'Shoot.'

'First I need some background to this project. And an overview of our itinerary and what you want me to do.'

'The idea is to help teens who come from abusive backgrounds, or who have been in prison, failed at school, and feel they have no future. The Cavershams aim to show them that they can stop the cycle, that they don't have to repeat their parents' mistakes and that their background does not have to define them. They can choose to walk away from the past, choose to leave the cycle of crime and move forward.'

'Breaking a cycle is tough—especially when that cycle involves your family. Sometimes it doesn't feel like there is a choice.'

'There is *always* a choice. However tough. However hefty the price tag.' He'd lost his family and it had nearly broken him, but it had been the choice he had made.

Give it a rest, Daniel.

Her green eyes were way too discerning.

'Anyway, it's an admirable cause. This trip is

about giving them new experiences and a chance to have fun. Using the wilderness to illustrate the power of nature, give them a different environment to the one they are used to. So that's an overview of what's happening in the Highlands. Venice is a whole different scenario.'

'What's our remit there?'

'The whole event is already organised—we will just need to double-check the details, sort out any last-minute glitches, host the ball and run the auction. Ethan and Ruby had planned to go, but they have had to change their plans.'

The Cavershams were adopting two children, a brother and a sister, and they were due to move in with them as soon as all the red tape and processes were completed.

Kaitlin nodded. 'Cora told me—they must be over the moon.'

'Yes.'

Try as he might he couldn't inject his voice with any enthusiasm, and she frowned.

'You don't believe in adoption?' Her perfect brows rose in a gesture that marked disapproval.

'I *do* believe in adoption—and I wish the

Cavershams well. But, speaking for myself, I don't believe in parenthood.'

'You don't want children?' The surprise in her voice was genuine.

'No, I don't.'

The idea of being a father caused him to break out in a cold sweat that had nothing to do with the late-evening sunshine that slanted through the restaurant's open sash windows.

'Too much responsibility.'

He'd seen what it had done to his own parents. His father had been so desperate to do his parental duty that he'd died before Daniel had even been born. Giovanni Romano had worked all hours in a bid to provide for his family, and exhaustion had caused him to fall asleep behind the wheel of a lorry—with fatal consequences.

Kaitlin watched him with eyes that combined judgement with question. 'Children are a huge responsibility, but I believe a worthwhile one.'

Daniel wondered if his father, killed in his prime, would have agreed. If it hadn't been for his unborn son he might well be alive today. It was a question he could never know the answer to, and guilt tinged the sadness that tightened his chest with a familiar ache.

Enough. Face forward.

'That is your prerogative. I'm happy to keep my life childfree.'

'Yet you don't strike me as someone who shirks responsibility. You certainly haven't skimped on hard work.' She looked down at her notebook. 'According to my research, ten years ago you established a small firm in the North of England. You are now CEO of a global law firm.'

'That's a different type of responsibility, and I've loved every minute of it. I grew the company regionally at first, then nationally, and recently it has become global through a process of partnerships, mergers and acquisitions. A key to my success has been successful branding, but also an ability to create and maintain true corporate spirit and a shared ethos.'

Pride warmed him—success was what drove him. That and a need to prove he could make it without the backing of the mob, a desire to show his mother *he* could provide for her.

He glanced across at Kaitlin, who scribbled industriously in her book. 'Why the research?'

'Because having some information about you enables me to know the right thing to say to different people. So, for example, if I know you love archery and I am speaking to a guest in Venice who also loves archery I can put you together.'

Daniel studied her expression—the small frown of concentration that crinkled her brow, the serious set of her lips. Clearly the conversational prowess she was known for came at a price, and he wondered if she did this before *any* conversation, public or private, if she always vetted each and every word.

'For the record, I've never done archery. I used to be a dab hand at basketball, and I've done some boxing, but nowadays I mostly work. I will admit to a love of food, though, and I like to cook. Does that help?'

'Yes. Thank you. Now, can you tell me the exact itinerary for the days in Scotland? What activities are we participating in? How many teenagers will be there?'

'Fifteen kids, aged from fifteen to nineteen. Nine boys, six girls. The first day we'll be kayaking, the next day hiking, the third day there will be a choice—' He broke off. 'Is there a problem?'

'No.'

'Then why have you gone pale?'

'It must be a trick of the light.'

Bending over the notebook, she appeared to be writing ferociously, but her fingers held the pen in a death grip and the pallor of her skin had nothing to do with the lighting.

She released the pen and looked over his shoulder. 'Here comes the main course.'

CHAPTER SIX

DESPITE THE INCREDIBLY appetising scent that
wafted up from their plates—garlic interlaced
with a touch of parsley and a tang of lemon—
foreboding touched Kaitlin. *Kayaking...* As if
everything wasn't bad enough already, she would
have to face a water-based activity. Water had always inspired her with unease, and it was a fear
her kidnappers had played upon—revealed to
them by the Derwent Manor staff member who
had help lure her to her capture.

After the kidnap that unease had matured into
a full-scale phobia, alongside a multitude of anx-
ieties that had had her seeing danger lurking at
each and every corner. But water had been the
worst... The idea of it dragging her down, of not
being able to breathe, had been too reminiscent
of what her captors had inflicted upon her. Black
terror as she'd been blindfolded, held under the

water and pulled out only when her lungs had teetered on the verge of collapse.

Anxiety unfurled tendril after tendril of fear that twisted her tummy into knots of apprehension.

'Earth to Kaitlin?'

The deep timbre of Daniel's voice pulled her back to reality.

Focus.

A glance down at her plate. The swirl of linguine. Rings of calamari. The vibrant red of tomato sauce patterned by tiny green capers. Next she looked at the pale gold of the white wine. Up to Daniel's face. Craggy, strong, intensity in his ice-blue eyes as they watched her, the formation of a frown on his forehead.

'Is everything OK?' he asked.

'Everything is fine.' The panic began to recede and she knew she had it under control. 'Why wouldn't it be?'

The attempt at lightness not quite pulled off.

'You've gone pale, and you zoned out for a couple of minutes there.'

Pride stiffened her spine—she would *not* admit

her fear to Mr Fearless over there. She would work this out. 'I have no idea what you mean.'

Daniel's blue eyes watched her with a scrutiny way too deep, whilst his lawyer instincts were no doubt limbering up.

'Something I've said has bothered you big-time and I want to know what it is. I am responsible for this project and I want it to work. So—spill.'

'It's not a problem, as such, but I've never kay-aked before and I don't want to make an absolute fool of myself.' Or expose her panic attacks to the eyes of the world. 'The thought of the press catching a candid camera shot of me tumbling into the water fills me with horror.'

'That hardly warrants your reaction.'

Think.

'Actually. it does. I told you. Image is everything.'

The Lady Kaitlin Derwent persona she'd built for herself relied on poise—she projected self-possession and people believed she was filled with an abundance of self-confidence. She couldn't afford a chink in that façade.

'I'd like to maintain mine.'

Because it was all she had. And if that made her look shallow so be it.

Twirling a forkful of linguine, she glanced down at her notebook. 'Next question—which hotel are we staying in?'

'We're not. One of the directors of the Caversham Foundation owns a cottage in Inverness—it happens to be empty now, so we'll stay there. It saves on costs and in actual fact will give us more privacy than a hotel.'

Just freaking fabulous. As if she wasn't sufficiently all over the place.

'That's a problem.' She'd been idiot enough to utter the words aloud. Clearly a breakdown was underway, because Lady Kaitlin did *not* blurt out foolish statements. 'I mean…from the perspective of the press, the less privacy the better. The whole point of this exercise is to scotch any hint of a rumour.'

'Exactly. In which case staying in a property offered to us for free makes sense. Declining it to stay in a hotel would look as if we *did* have something to hide. It's all arranged—to change it now would arouse way more suspicion.'

Kaitlin picked up her wine glass and took a

healthy slug—this whole scenario got worse and worse as each course progressed.

'OK. Fine. But, for the record, I believe it is a mistake.'

'Noted. Next question...'

And the next and the next...

By the end of dinner her hand threatened to cramp but hopefully she had enough information to stave off panic.

'Thank you for this. It has really helped.'

She scraped up the last bit of tiramisu from her bowl, savoured the gossamer lightness of the lady's fingers kissed with the tang of espresso.

'You're welcome. I'll walk you home and then pick you up tomorrow to take you to the airport.'

Fifteen hours later Daniel observed Kaitlin's study of the private jet. 'I didn't realise we would be travelling by private jet.'

'A company perk. I can't tell if you disapprove or if you are relieved.'

'A bit of both. It does seem morally wrong that we'll be taking these teenagers into the wilds and yet we're imposing this massive carbon footprint on the environment. On the other hand we will avoid the crowds and the publicity, and today that suits me.'

Presumably because she was tired, Daniel thought. Despite her trademark elegance, show-cased in a patterned dress that combined tur-quoise and red and was worn, he suspected, to divert attention from the smudges under her eyes—eyes that had dulled to a flat, almost lack-lustre green.

Yet he sensed that if they had been on a char-tered flight she would have sparkled, chatting with ease to anyone who recognised her, flight attendants and squalling children alike.

'The way I see it is that this brings us privacy and convenience. I like it.'

'So is this how you *always* travel?'

'A fair amount. I travel a lot, and it's useful to be able to utilise the time to work. It's what a lot of corporate clients expect as well—and, as someone once told me, image is everything.'

This pulled a smile from her. 'If the image you're trying to project is one of success, you've nailed it. My bet is that you have a sports car in your garage and the clothes you are wearing set you back a hefty sum. Though you've gone for discreet quality over brash designer label.'

'Was the car a guess or research?' He nodded at the ubiquitous notebook that rested on the table in front of her, close to hand, almost like a talisman.

'It was a guess. Though there *is* some more research I'd like to do.'

His eyebrows rose of their own volition as he eyed the notebook with more than a hint of fascination 'There can't possibly be any more questions to ask.'

'There is always more information to collect. I assume you research before you go to court? This is the same idea. It's my job. If you want this project to get good publicity then I have to work out the best way to do that—my strategy, how I will project Lady Kaitlin to maximise benefit. So it's important I wear the right outfit, say the right thing at the right time.'

'Fair enough.' Yet a good few of the questions the previous night had been about their destination, the exact location of the kayaking school, the website for the cottage in Inverness and the hotel in Venice… Surely irrelevant for publicity purposes. 'So what else do you want to know?'

'How to handle the kids.' Her gaze met his, fair and square. 'I want to figure out how to relate to the teenagers—find a frame of reference.' Her slender fingers tapped the notebook. 'I come from a wealthy, privileged background, so these teenagers may well resent me. I'm looking for a way round that. If you come from a similar background you may have some ideas how to combat that.'

Discomfort scratched his skin at the knowledge that his privileged upbringing, the wealth that had cushioned his childhood, the expensive education, had all come from the proceeds of crime. True, he'd funded his own way through law school, through sheer hard graft, but that didn't cancel out the sting of guilt.

Kaitlin huffed out a sigh. 'Actually, scrub that. However you started out, you've clearly worked damned hard to get where you are. The kids will respect that. But they will see that I was born to wealth and position and have done nothing to earn it. I'm worried my presence may goad them, make them feel patronised, especially because I'm not sure what I can offer them.'

Despite her matter-of-fact tone, he could sense the tremor of vulnerability and it touched him. 'You earn a living. You have a job. Tell me about it.'

'I work in an art gallery. I liaise with customers and artists. I help decide who we represent. I organise promotional events and I am the "face" of the gallery.'

'So you have a knowledge of art, an ability to sell and to interact with people—not to mention organisational skills. There is plenty there to earn respect. You can discuss art and painting. Hell, you may spark an interest that means some teenager goes on to become the next Picasso.'

For a second her green eyes were luminous with wist. 'Perhaps. But it's a job that was given to me because the owner knows my mother and likes the kudos of having a "Lady" working for her.'

'Is it a job you wanted?'

'It was a job that was presented to me and that fits in with my duties to Derwent Manor, and I'm good at it.'

'That doesn't answer my question.'

Daniel frowned. With Kaitlin's intelligence, connections, looks and personality she could surely have pursued any career she wanted?

'I didn't know what I wanted to do, so this seemed as suitable as anything else. Did you always know you wanted to be a lawyer?'

'Yes.'

Perhaps because once he'd understood what had happened to his father he'd been able to see the burning injustice of it all.

Giovanni Romano's family had disowned him for marrying Daniel's mother. Part of that rejection had entailed sacking him from his job in the family business. The young Daniel had wondered what would have happened if his parents had consulted a lawyer, found grounds for unfair dismissal. Then there had been his father's subsequent contract to drive a lorry. The young Daniel had been sure there must be some flaw in it—perhaps too many hours, some kind of exploitation, something that the law would have found. That way his father's death when he'd crashed the lorry through sheer exhaustion would have been prevented.

Daniel wiped a hand down his face, swiped the memory away. History could not be rewritten, and in the here and now it was Kaitlin who intrigued him. 'I did. But don't change the subject. We were talking about *you*. You must have had some idea of what you wanted to do.'

'Nope. I didn't. I did well at school, but nothing inspired me.' Her green eyes widened, as if she was looking back to a past that held less than stellar memories. She shrugged. 'I guess I have no ambition.'

'Except to marry well?'

'That's my parents' ambition—not mine,' she flashed back, and then pressed her lips together in clear self-irritation. 'The point is that I do not have any burning career drive.'

'You must have had a childhood dream. Everyone does.'

'Of course.' Her hand waved in a dismissive gesture. 'As a child I believed I could do anything. Thought I could pick between doctor, singer, dancer, scientist…you name it, I'd imagined it.'

Daniel's frown deepened. It didn't make sense that she'd gone from being a motivated, ambitious kid to someone who had drifted into a job that clearly did not set her world on fire.

'Then look around. You're twenty-seven years old—the world is your oyster. You can still be a dancer, a singer, a doctor or a scientist. That's the message we want to give those teenagers—that no matter what your background you need to strive to be what you want to be. It doesn't matter if it's a lawyer or a shop assistant—it needs to give you satisfaction.'

Kaitlin's expression shuttered and she glanced away, out of the window, just as the pilot announced their descent. 'I'll do my best to get that message across.'

The other message she had best get across to herself was to stop talking—*cease conversation* with Daniel. Perhaps it was the lawyer in him, but the man had an uncanny knack of extracting information from her she had no wish to share. Somehow her lips opened and out came the words; she pitied any witness who came up against him.

Which was exactly why she had feigned sleep for the entire car journey from the airport to their destination. A location she had spent a considerable time researching—enough so that she knew she'd need to filter out the background noise of the Caledonian Canal that ran along the edge of the spacious garden that graced the property.

Instead, as she alighted from the car with a theatrical stretch that Daniel surveyed with a scepticism that suggested he had seen straight through the fake nap, she focused on the cottage itself.

Lush vegetation nestled around white walls that gleamed bright through the mizzle of rain that hazed the air and contrasted with the dark orange of the roof, whilst large glass windows indicated that the inside would prove spacious and light.

'It's even prettier than the photographs on the website.'

Pictures Kaitlin had studied until her eyeballs ached in the knowledge that the more prepared she was the more likely it was she could stave off panic. It was a strategy that worked—as they entered she felt in control, with not so much as a twinge of nerves daring to show.

'I asked for food to be left for us, so there won't be a need to go out unless you want to,' Daniel said as they entered the well-equipped kitchen.

'Nope. Sounds great. I'm happy to stay in.'

At least in theory. In reality the idea of staying in with Daniel made her feel…jittery, and awareness slid over her skin.

Both stood frozen to the linoleum floor, eyes locked, until Daniel spun on his heel in an abrupt movement and headed to the fridge, yanked it open with a jerk.

'Yup, plenty of provisions. I could make us a three-cheese omelette with ham, or spaghetti carbonara? Your choice. Unless you want to cook?'

'Cooking isn't one of my talents—so an omelette sounds great, if you don't mind.'

'No problem. It'll be ready in half an hour.'

'Great.' Which was apparently her new word for the evening.

Goodness knew she needed that thirty minutes to think, to work out how to get through a cosy, domestic dinner without disgrace.

A shower and a change of clothes undoubtedly

helped. Ruffle edged shirt tucked into smart casual black trousers cinched at the waist with a simple buckled brown belt. The ensemble would hopefully ditch any semblance of 'cosy' and the near severity of her chignon, softened by the release of only a few stray tendrils of hair, conveyed business.

One final deep breath and she entered the kitchen, from where a truly tantalising scent wafted, along with the strains of a classical music radio station.

'That smells glorious.'

'Thank you. Help yourself to wine.'

'Great.'

Really, Kaitlin? Get yourself a thesaurus.

Opening the fridge, she located an open bottle of white wine and poured herself a glass. 'Can I help?'

'You can set the table.'

'No problem.'

A surreal feeling hit her as she carefully arranged placemats and cutlery, carried the blue glass salad bowl heaped with spinach, its dark green leaves sprinkled with shavings of parmesan, to the square wooden table. She was trying to convince her brain that this was no different from a business dinner—it was only the setting that gave it this false sense of domesticity.

Yet once she was seated her brain scrambled for *any* conversational topic, and for once in her life came up short. It seemed as if Daniel was suffering from a similar affliction, and she could only be thankful for the music, which was at least filling the void of silence.

This was ridiculous—the entire concept of social awkwardness was an impossibility to Kaitlin. She had not spent years of her life perfecting her conversational skills to be beaten by this. Whatever *this* was.

Pressing her lips together, she considered the options. Clearly she needed to re-arm herself, pull her Lady Kaitlin persona together and keep it together. Somehow Daniel Harrington had messed with her head—and that had to be because of this unwanted physical attraction, this stupid hum that she had never felt before and needed to eradicate or at the very least neutralise.

'Penny for them?'

Daniel's deep voice broke her reverie and she

glanced up. 'They aren't worth it. I'm sure *your* thoughts would be far more interesting.'

That was better.

'I'm not sure that is the adjective I'd use.'

Uh-oh. There was an amused tone to his voice—a glint in his eye that sent a skitter of heat along her veins.

'What adjective *would* you use?'

'Inappropriate probably best covers it.'

'Oh.' There was no textbook answer to that.

'Don't worry—I am not about to act on my thoughts, but perhaps we need to clear the air? So that we can get on with what we are here to do—focus on the teenagers.'

'OK. You first.'

He pushed his empty plate away and picked up his wine. 'I'm still attracted to you. A lot. But it doesn't have to be a big deal.'

'But it *is* a big deal to me.' Kaitlin closed her eyes in silent despair; disbelief rippling through her at her blurted words even as her mind raced to think how to explain them. 'Because…because it feels awkward.'

'"Awkward" as in you feel embarrassed or uncomfortable? Or "awkward" as in the attraction still exists?'

With a supreme effort she forced her brain into gear, shut down the idiotic thrill that surged through her bloodstream at the knowledge that he felt the same attraction. *Big-time.*

Thrill or not, it made life too complicated. One-sided attraction was bad—mutual attraction was disastrous. So she'd opt for a strategy that had served her well. Good old denial.

'For me, the attraction no longer exists—Barcelona was an aberration that makes me feel both embarrassed and uncomfortable.'

The sheer scale of the lie was immense, but she kept her gaze on his, channelled every fibre of Lady Kaitlin and hoped her body language was on point.

'I just want to get through this week and move on.'

Daniel was silent. Then he lifted his shoulders in another shrug. 'I acknowledge that I misread the situation and I apologise if I have caused you embarrassment.'

'Thank you.' Guilt touched her, along with a

sense of profound regret. 'I'll help clear up and then I'll head to my room.'

Kaitlin opened her eyes, stared up at the off-white Artex ceiling. Where *was* she? A feeling of panic invaded but she headed it off at the pass, studied the swirls and whorls of the plaster and allowed knowledge to seep in. Fort William. Scotland. She was safe.

The belated beep of her alarm was a reminder that she had set up a kayaking lesson, in the hope that it would prevent any unseemly panic the following day.

She swung her legs out of bed and picked her phone up from the pine chest of drawers that doubled as a bedside cabinet. Taxi called, bathroom utilised, she donned the outfit she'd set out the previous night on the square-backed cream armchair tucked in the room's corner. Jeans, T-shirt, a plain white shirt and a dark blue lightweight knit jumper provided the layers recommended.

Half an hour later she exited the house, relieved that there was no sight nor sound of Daniel, and twenty minutes after that she stood at the meeting point.

Her head told her to feast her eyes on the scenery—the vibrant green foliage, the backdrop of dense rolling woodland—to breathe deeply of the scent of heather and gorse that sprinkled the air.

But her gaze kept being pulled inexorably back to the water, and the sight of it caused her heart to make a spirited attempt to leap from her chest. Her lungs constricted and little black dots danced the tango on her retinas.

Breathe.

She could do this—she *would* do this. And after tomorrow she need never ever go anywhere near water again unless it was in the safety of a bathroom.

'Kaitlin?'

The deep voice from behind her lasered her body into immobility. It couldn't be…

Forcing her feet to uproot themselves, she spun round and blinked at Daniel. 'Daniel? What are you doing here?'

There was a frown on his face and his mouth

was set to grim. 'Why didn't you tell me about this lesson?'

'As far as I know I don't have to account for every minute of my day with you. Where's Matt?'

'I told him I'd take the lesson.'

Oh, great! She really wasn't sure she could deal with this overload of sensation. Panic at the proximity of the water battled with panic at the proximity of Daniel. The idea of the two combining made implosion viable.

One thing at a time, Kaitlin.

'Why?'

'I don't want it to be awkward just because I misread the signals.'

His blue eyes met hers with an unreadable expression and in that instant she wondered if he believed her.

'I thought if I took you out in the kayak it might ease things. But of course if you would prefer Matt I'll call him.'

Now what?

Digging deep, she turned back to face the water—and realised that, like it or not, his presence made her feel safe.

'If you're sure you don't mind, then let's start this lesson.'

With a brief nod he retreated, returning with two brightly coloured kayaks that he took down to the water's edge.

'OK. So here's what you need to know before we start…'

His words were concise and easy to understand as he explained safety procedures and helped her into a life jacket. But as they edged nearer to the moment where she would actually have to go into the boat on the water it became harder and harder to concentrate as she fought back fear and kept it at bay.

'Are you ready?'

'Sure.' If she didn't count clammy skin and leaden limbs. 'Just a bit nervous about actually getting into the kayak.'

The bright red-trimmed boat looked ridiculously small and outrageously fragile as it bobbed up and down.

'That can be one of the trickiest things. Don't forget what I said about bending your knees deeply, so you can get into a good low squat.

That way your centre of gravity is low and you achieve stability. I'll go first and you watch.'

As he squatted down her gaze couldn't help but be snagged on the sheer strength of his torso, the power of his thighs, and for a welcome instant appreciation cut clean through her anxiety for enough precious seconds that she could manage to follow suit once he was in.

There. She was in the kayak and it would keep her afloat as long as she could focus on Daniel's instructions.

The best way to do that was to imagine the water away, fantasise that she was in the gym and focus on Daniel's tuition about how to grasp the paddle, the angle of manoeuvre, the different techniques of bracing, rolling, turning… All verbs that her tummy took as instruction even as she exerted every bit of Lady Kaitlin to demonstrate not an iota of her inner chaos.

'Brilliant! There you go. You're a natural.'

The reassurance of his voice allowed her to focus on getting through. If she didn't look at the water…if she continued the pretence that she was on a rowing machine and concentrated on the movement of the paddle…

Twenty minutes later a sudden cautious thrill of pride shot through her, and the unfamiliar feeling caught her by surprise. When was the last time she'd felt proud of herself or stepped out of her comfort zone?

For one treacherous second she revelled in the feeling and forgot the whole pretence that she was safely ensconced in a gym in Chelsea. The scenery flashed into view: the shoreline in the distance, the expanse of the canal around her, the tug of the current that rocked the boat as she lost the paddle's rhythm…

Debilitating panic struck. All pride, all her joy in her accomplishment shattered into shards of terror. The metallic taste of fear coated her tongue as she stared mesmerised into the looming menace of the water.

Common sense made an attempt to cleave through the fear—told her she had a life jacket on, that she was not in a storm-tossed sea.

But it made no headway against the inner hurricane of irrational panic that swept through her body and her mind. The pounding in her ears, the throbbing of her heart and an all too familiar clamminess swamped the voice of reason and refused to allow the tips and strategies garnered from her internet searches and research over the years to permeate.

The paddle fell from her hand and she tried to grip the side of the kayak, tried to remember how to breathe through the haze that clogged her lungs. The craft rocked and toppled and over she went, the ice cold shock of the water intensifying the nightmare.

'Kaitlin!'

The deep, authoritative sound of Daniel's voice reverberated faintly and she dimly registered a splash. Then his arms were around her. For an instant blind fear kicked her into fight or flight mode—images of her thirteen-year-old self filled her mind. Being picked up and bundled into the boot of the car, the struggle, the sickly scent of something clamped to her mouth, the wrench of pain... Being held over the water, submerged...

Then... 'Kaitlin. It's Daniel. I've got you. Trust me.'

Trust.

No, she couldn't.

'Just stop fighting and I'll let you go. The life jacket will buoy you up. You're safe.'

Slowly his voice had an effect, and she concentrated on the cold, the sensation of his arms around her.

Daniel. Daniel.

This was the here and now—not years ago. No one was trying to take her, force her... Slowly her brain kicked back into gear, pulled her into the present.

Do your breathing exercises—in and out, count to five. *Open your eyes and focus on your surroundings.* On the craggy contours of Daniel's features, the water-drenched dark hair, one curl sculpted to his brow, the intense blue of his eyes, the outline of his mouth...

Muzzy warning bells rang but she ignored them, too caught in the moment as anxiety morphed into heightened sensations of an entirely different kind. Awareness soared inside her, oblivious to the layers of clothing that separated them, to the ice-cold of the water. On some level it occurred to her that it was the surroundings she should focus on—the towering height of the pines, the bulk of the mountains in the distance, the call of a kestrel as it swooped in the sky, the kayaks bobbing gently away from them—but it all faded against his aura that projected sheer strength and safety. Made her want to remain in his hold.

Think.

But thought was nigh on impossible when an answering awareness dawned in his eyes...when he was so close...when all she wanted to do was reach up and cup the jut of his jaw...

Stop!

Any minute reporters might converge on the shore—and, more than that, Daniel represented danger. He made it harder to be the person she wanted to be—Lady Kaitlin Derwent.

So from somewhere deep inside she summoned reserves of strength. 'We need to get the kayaks. I'm all right now.'

Not entirely true, the icy fingers of water still made unease flare, but she could control it. *Would* control it.

'They aren't too far away.'

'Are you sure you're OK?' he asked.

'Yes.' But her teeth had started to chatter

now, and a wave of tiredness descended as he released her.

Telling herself she'd be fine, she watched as he retrieved the kayaks and returned.

'Let's get you back in.'

The soothing tone of his voice, the confidence that he would be able to do just that, gave her the impetus to follow his instructions, and relief hit as soon as she was in the relative safety of the kayak.

'I'll be right beside you.'

Kaitlin nodded, gritted her teeth and focused on the paddle, on their movement to the shoreline and what it represented. Finally they arrived, and she scrambled out onto dry land.

'Let's get you home and out of—' He broke off and his lips turned up in a rueful smile. 'You need to warm up.'

Kaitlin managed a nod, and could only be thankful Daniel wasn't a mind-reader as her treacherous brain took the idea of being taken out of her clothes and warmed up and ran with it.

Stop it.

This was nothing more than a reaction to the panic attack. 'Let's go.'

CHAPTER SEVEN

TWO HOURS LATER Daniel rose as Kaitlin entered the tastefully furnished comfortable lounge, where a medley of cream and red sofas and overstuffed armchairs were arranged against a backdrop of Scottish landscapes and a vista of the real live Caledonian Canal seen through the enormous wall-wide windows.

Kaitlin walked across the room with her customary grace, all trace of panic eradicated. Her slightly damp hair fell in a sleek Titian curtain to touch her shoulders, and she wore a simply cut white blouse edged with lace over a pair of jeans. She looked gorgeous and exuded a clean, flowery smell he couldn't identify but which teased his nostrils.

Desire made him almost groan out loud, and it took every ounce of his will to keep him standing still. Kaitlin had made it clear she wasn't interested, and whilst his experience told him her body wasn't fully on board with that decision it wasn't in his psyche to force an admission of attraction.

Anyway, getting involved with Kaitlin was a bad, bad idea. Stupid on all levels. It would embroil him in a media hype he truly didn't want. But also Kaitlin was too complicated—he still couldn't fathom the reasons for her deception in Barcelona, and he sensed the existence of baggage that he should have no desire to open.

Yet for some reason he wanted to know what made her tick, and that was a mistake—the first footfall on a slippery path. Curiosity would lead to entanglement and the formation of bonds, however tenuous—ties that would have the potential to bind or, perhaps worse, to be broken. Either way, pain was the result.

There it was again—the grief etched on his mother's face when he'd left. Grief *he* had caused.

So any form of involvement with Kaitlin was a no-go zone. His cardinal relationship rule— keep it clean, simple and short-term—needed to remain inviolate.

'Feeling better?'

'Yes. Thank you.'

'You should have told me you were scared of water.'

Kaitlin lifted her shoulders and the sudden weariness on her face touched him with compassion.

'I hoped it would be OK…that the phobia would have gone.'

'How long have you had it?'

Her reluctance to answer was palpable in the way she smoothed her hands down her jeans, but then she turned to face him, held his gaze with an aloofness that he believed to be her best defence method.

'A few years.' A shadow darkened the green of her eyes to jade.

'Have you seen anyone about it?'

'No need. It's not like I have a yen to swim the Channel. I can manage it. I *will* manage it.'

Her voice was cool and determined, and if he hadn't witnessed her panic attack earlier he would have believed her without question,

'Uh-uh.' Daniel shook his head. 'Not on my watch. No way are you kayaking tomorrow.'

'Yes, I am. The whole point of today was to prepare me for tomorrow.'

Admiration touched him that she was willing to put herself through the ordeal again, but he shook his head. 'Not necessary.'

'Yes, it is. I will *not* let this phobia win—I can't.'

The grit in her voice, the starkness of her tone indicated a depth to Lady Kaitlin he hadn't realised existed.

'I made a commitment to this exercise and I will honour it. The whole point of my presence is to bring publicity to the campaign. I can't do that if I'm not there.'

'It's not the publicity I'm concerned about. It's you.'

'Oh.'

Her forehead scrunched in surprise—almost as if it hadn't occurred to her that anyone could be concerned for her on a personal level.

'That's…that's very kind of you.' The words were stilted, and as if she realised it she paused to regroup. 'But truly there's no need. I will be fine. I *want* to do this, Daniel. Please.'

The low entreaty tugged at his chest and he

thought quickly. 'OK. But we'll go in a tandem kayak. You and I.'

You and I.

For some reason the words held a strange sonorous significance. Ridiculous—this was no more than a practical solution.

'And if there is any sign of panic you'll tell me. Promise?'

'I promise.' Her green eyes met his with a hint of shyness. 'Thank you.'

'No problem.'

The silence stretched and twanged as awareness hovered in the air. Daniel forced his feet to remain rooted to the cream-carpeted floor, curbed the impulse that had him wanting to close the gap between them, pull her into his arms and kiss her.

Bad idea, Dan.

Though right here and now he was having a hard time remembering why.

Kaitlin seemed equally lost for conversation, but then she gave a small shake of her head and clenched her fingers into her palms. 'So, what are your plans for the rest of the day?'

'To hike over the walk we're taking the kids

on. It's a beautiful trek, and I want the chance to scope it out first.' Before his brain could cut in, his mouth ran away with him. 'Would you like to come?'

Yet another bad idea. Instinct told him that the less time he spent alone with Kaitlin the better. But after her ordeal he didn't want to leave her alone, so common politeness had dictated the invitation—nothing more. Common sense would ensure non-involvement.

There was a second of hesitation and then Kaitlin nodded. 'I'd like that.' A small frown creased her forehead. 'I prefer to be prepared, so I appreciate this. Plus I'll get to break in my new hiking boots and check that I can actually manage the hike.'

Deep breath.

'I'll go and get ready.'

Kaitlin gazed at her reflection in the mirror, then leant her forehead against the cool glass in the hope it would bring her back to her senses. She should never have agreed to the walk—her second favourite strategy after denial was avoidance. Ergo, she should duck, sidestep, positively *dodge* any time with Daniel.

But it would help to check out the hike, and she *was* Lady Kaitlin Derwent, and she was in control.

Twenty minutes later, having pulled on hiking socks and what she hoped would prove to be state-of-the-art walking boots, she went in search of Daniel and found him in the kitchen, loading up a rucksack.

'I've packed us a picnic,' he explained. 'We'll drive to Fort William, park in town and walk from there.'

As Kaitlin climbed into the gleaming black four-wheel drive she glanced across at Daniel. His concentration on the road allowed her to watch the deft confidence with which he drove, the economical movements, the shape of his hands, the… *Enough.* She should be feasting her eyes on the landscape outside, not Daniel's fingers, for heaven's sake.

And so for the rest of the short car journey Kaitlin watched the many shades of green and brown morph together into rolling meadows and plains, backed by mountainous peaks and tors, until they arrived at the bustling town of Fort William, one of the largest in the Highlands.

Kaitlin inhaled deeply, reminded herself that it was no different from London—less familiar, but in many essentials the same—and the sight of familiar High Street brands grounded her as they drove through the town and parked.

They alighted from the car and left the car park behind them, and soon they were following the zig-zag path uphill, leaving the noise of traffic and the hustle behind until it was nigh on impossible to believe the proximity of a town that housed thousands of people.

The air was fresh and the crisp breeze carried the scent of the Highlands...gorse, heather with an evocative nuance of peat and whisky... After they'd scaled a small summit they paused, and Kaitlin stared out over the view and felt a sense of peace descend on her. The travails of the day, the terror the water had invoked, were paradoxically soothed by the enormity of nature.

'I can see why you want to bring the kids here,' she said. 'All of this is timeless—makes you feel that no matter what is happening in the cities, in our lives...all the progress, all the fears…when you set it against this it gives you a certain peace.'

Whoa—the plan had been to focus on small talk, to push Daniel into the realms of acquaintance. Instead she was waxing lyrical with philosophy.

Before he could answer she turned away. 'Where next?'

The curved path led into a woodland area, where alder, willow and birch lined their ascent, and emerged to a view of a bulky hill—a foothill of Ben Nevis. Kaitlin paused and eyed the windy, steep peat path with trepidation.

Daniel raised his eyebrows. 'Worried you won't make it?'

In actual fact she'd been worried that her panic might make yet another show. But the challenge in his voice, delivered with a note of teasing and accompanied by a half-smile that notched up her heartbeat, helped shut down the fear before it could take hold.

'Not in the slightest. I may not be an outdoorsy girl, but I keep fit.'

'Then let's go. And I promise the views will be worth it.'

Lord knew he wasn't wrong—but she'd be a liar if she didn't admit, at least to herself, that the view she focused on most was the contours of his muscular body, the lithe strength of his frame, the length of his leg, the breadth of his thigh… Until they reached the top, where the panoramic stretch of moorland took her breath away.

Daniel halted. 'I don't know about you, but I am famished. Shall we stop for lunch?'

'Sure.'

He shrugged off the rucksack, unstrapped it, tugged out a tartan picnic blanket and spread it on the ground. Kaitlin sat, her eyes widening as he pulled out item after item. Long baguettes, a selection of cheese, pâté, small pies lidded with smooth pastry edges…

'It's like a magic rucksack.'

'I hope you're hungry?'

'Actually, I am. It must be the fresh air and the exercise. There is obviously a big difference between walking on a treadmill and out in the real world!'

Silence fell as they busied themselves, and it was only once their plates were laden that

Kaitlin applied her mind to conversation. There would be no more awkward silences bridged by growing awareness.

'Is this the type of holiday you usually have? Or are you more the party-on-a-yacht type of guy?'

'I'm not big on holidays. I travel plenty with work, so I usually combine a weekend away with business.'

'So Ethan must have been very persuasive to get you to do this?'

'He was.' He stretched his legs out and balanced his plate. 'What about you? Where do you holiday?'

Kaitlin shrugged. 'Like you, I'm not a holiday person. The last time I tried to go with friends it turned into a publicity fest and it was ruined for them.'

But in reality that was an excuse—she didn't enjoy holidays. New places overwhelmed her, and the effort it took to research and find a new routine mostly wasn't worth it.

'Is must be hard to be on show all the time.'

'It's part of what I do and I'm good at it.'

'But surely any publicity intrusive enough to stop you going on holiday is too much?'

'It doesn't bother me. We never holidayed as children, so holidays have never been part of my life.' Her parents wouldn't have known where to begin—Derwent Manor had always been their priority. 'My parents thought it a waste of money.'

Daniel raised his eyebrows as he spread a wedge of pâté onto a cracker. 'I didn't think money was an issue for the Derwents.'

'That's what most people think. In reality Derwent Manor absorbs huge amounts of money every year in maintenance alone, Then we had a flood a few years back, and that caused extensive damage, and so it goes on. Most of my school holidays were spent fundraising.'

'Did you mind?'

'No.'

The idea of a Derwent family holiday was impossible even to imagine—any attempt and the illusion shimmered and wisped away. The Duke and Duchess had always parented from a distance, and with Kaitlin that distance had been touched with their distaste after the kidnap—

as if she were soiled goods. Though they had still shown her way more attention and approval than they had ever given Cora, but on the flip-side that had meant their expectations of Lady Kaitlin were correspondingly higher.

Shaking the thoughts off, Kaitlin bit into a piece of quiche and savoured the tart cheddar taste. 'What about you? What sort of holidays did you go on as a child?'

For a moment she thought he wouldn't answer; his blue eyes were looking past her towards the line of the horizon, as if he could see into the past. Then…

'Big, noisy, fun ones. We'd take off to the beach for weeks. My stepdad and brother would bar-becue up a storm and the rest of us kids would run riot.'

'How many of you were there?'

'Me, my brother and sister, and a whole bunch of cousins.'

'That sounds amazing.'

'It was a long time ago.'

His voice heavy with bleakness, and what she instinctively knew was a mix of nostalgia and regret, and without even thinking she reached out and touched his arm.

'But you have the memories. We don't have any cousins—it's just the three of us, and Cora, Gabe and I weren't that close as children—we aren't a close family. It sounds like you were.' She hesitated. 'Maybe you still could be?'

Daniel shook his head. 'It didn't work out like that.' The words were uttered with a finality that indicated the subject was closed. 'Sounds like you've done better—you seem close to Gabe and Cora now.'

'We're closer than we used to be.'

He reached for a bottle of water, his gaze curious but without condemnation. 'You aren't close to your parents and yet you were happy to marry a man they chose for you?'

Kaitlin knew she should close the conversation down, but sitting out there, with the spring breeze wafting the scent of heather, surrounded by peace, she wanted him to understand. Perhaps she needed to explain it to herself.

'It's more complicated than that. I was born to the job of being Lady Kaitlin Derwent and the responsibilities that come with that. When I was little that meant posing for photo shoots in cute outfits or behaving at boring dinner parties.'

'And now those obligations include marriage to a man of your parents' choosing? That's the high jump and the pole vault combined.'

'Not if I loathed him—I wouldn't let them force me into marriage then…of course I wouldn't. But…'

But her parents had always made clear to her that it was her destiny to make a great alliance, to bring glory to the Derwent name. Once she had had other ideas, Deep inside herself she had been sure she was destined for other things, had vowed she would show her parents that she could bring glory to the Derwent name in a different way. Her options had seemed endless—she'd become a famous dancer, a Nobel prize-winning scientist, a brilliant pop singer…

With the kidnap all those aspirations had withered away.

'But…?' he prompted.

'But the idea of a husband like Frederick didn't seem like such a bad prospect. I would have done my best to be a good princess.' Placing her plate on the tartan rug, she enumerated the points on her fingers. 'I know how to garner positive publicity, I would be loyal, always look the part, always say the right thing.' A surge of confidence bolstered her against the incredulity on Daniel's face. 'I would be in a position to do good—I could make significant contributions to causes I believe in.'

'Stop.' Daniel raised a hand, the frown on his face now deeper. 'Everything you have said is about your role as Princess. What about your *actual* marriage? The nitty-gritty of real life?'

Of course she had considered that. 'I would do my best to be a good wife. I'd—'

'You'd pose nicely for the photographs? Look the part and always say the right thing?'

The sarcastic inflexion was harsh enough to make her flinch.

'Yes. There's nothing wrong with that.'

'*Everything* is wrong with that. You propose to play a part for your whole life. What about the parts that aren't acted out for the camera?'

Heat burned her cheeks and she focused on the baguette she held, crumbled it into a small mountain. 'I would do my best in private as well. But I don't think physical attraction matters.'

Daniel stared at her. 'Doesn't matter?' he echoed, his expression dumbfounded.

'There is a lot more to marriage than physical attraction.'

'Granted—but I think it is a fairly vital component.'

'Physical attraction can be a short-term illusion—marriage is for the long haul.'

'Exactly. That means the rest of your life.' His voice was slow now, imbued with urgency. 'If you are doing this for your parents you shouldn't. This is *your* life and you only get one shot. Don't waste it by living it any other way than the way you want to.'

'Marriage *is* what I want. I want security, companionship, and most of all I want children.'

For the first time in this conversation she felt solid ground beneath her—she knew that, however impossible romantic love was for her, her love for her children would be absolute.

'You don't have to marry a prince to have children. You could marry someone you love.'

'I don't want love. It's too unpredictable—too unreliable, too intangible.' Kaitlin wanted to put her trust in the tangible. 'That's why the idea of an alliance appeals to me. There would be a mutual contract to fulfil...agreed expectations.'

'What would *you* expect from *him*?'

'Liking, respect, that he's a good father to our children. Kindness. It works for me.'

Enough said—time to move this conversation away from her, before she revealed even more than she already had.

'What would work for *you*?'

Daniel blinked in surprise.

Kaitlin's eyes narrowed. 'We've discussed *my* attitude to long-term relationships—now it's your turn.'

'That's simple. Avoid them like the plague and avian flu rolled together. I'm not a "long-term" sort of guy.'

'Maybe you haven't met the right woman yet?'

'I have no intention of ever staying with a woman long enough to discover her eligibility as Ms Right. That's why I only date women on the lookout for a quick physical fling. A night here, a weekend there...'

A flush touched her face. 'Like in Barcelona?'

'Yes. Although I don't usually pick up strangers in hotel lobbies.'

Though that wasn't the reason that Barcelona had been different—'Lynette' had been a diversion from the stark realisation that his family would not accept his extended olive branch, that there would be no reunion or forgiveness or understanding.

'My usual dates are women I meet through work, on business trips or through colleagues. All are women I like and respect. But, unlike you, I don't think that's enough to warrant marriage. I have no wish to swap my bachelor lifestyle for the proverbial ball and chain. Too claustrophobic.'

A few years back he had tried a relationship, dated without a cut-off point, and it hadn't worked out. The minute the relationship had veered even slightly towards serious it had felt like the equivalent of a noose round his neck, and every day the rope had got that little bit tighter... the walls had closed in a little bit more...another barrier had gone up. Pick the analogy, but he'd learnt the lesson.

'There's always divorce.'

'Not straightforward. The desire to split might not be mutual, there could be children to consider, alongside a tangle of assets and emotions and mess, and someone will always get hurt.'

No matter what.

His mother had loved his father with all her heart and had been devastated by his death. Her subsequent marriage to his stepdad had been a supposed 'alliance', and that had been charged with misery. Lesson learnt. Love, marriage, kids, closeness were all to be avoided—too messy, too painful, too fraught.

'Better to avoid the whole shebang.'

'But my way avoids hurt and achieves a partnership that will run on an even keel.'

No doubt that was what his mother had believed.

'You can't control emotion. There is a possibility that one or both of you may fall for someone else.'

'I wouldn't.' There was certainty in her voice. 'I'm not coded that way.'

'Maybe your husband would.'

'He wouldn't. I'd do everything in my power to be the wife he wanted.'

'It doesn't always work like that.'

'I'll cross that bridge if I get to it.'

'And tolerate infidelity?'

Kaitlin pressed her lips together. 'I don't know. Maybe if it made him happy…maybe if it didn't hurt me…'

'You cannot possibly believe that. Infidelity humiliates you in your own right *and* in the eyes of your children. Regardless of whether you love your partner or not.'

There was a pause and he knew he'd screwed up—Kaitlin made a pastime of reading people— watching their every nuance and inflexion.

'You know that as fact, don't you?' she said.

What the hell? If it showed her the stupidity of her beliefs… 'Yes, I do. My stepfather cheated on my mother on numerous occasions and she turned a blind eye. But it destroyed her inside.'

It was the price she'd paid to remain inside her gilded cage, to keep her children by her. Her defence had been the fact that as long as she accepted infidelity Antonio Russo would never divorce her. But, oh, how Daniel had loathed it. The taste of bitterness still flavoured his memories. He still felt the twist of frustrated anger at his own helplessness.

Even now his fists clenched involuntarily at the memory. Never would he risk that kind of humiliation—one that would be even worse if you actually loved the other person.

'I'm sorry. I...'

'Don't be. But don't delude yourself either.'

With a savage gesture he pulled the rucksack towards him.

'We should move on.'

CHAPTER EIGHT

KAITLIN STARED AT her reflection the following morning and tried to push the memory of that foolish conversation from her mind. Disbelief lingered and mingled with irritation that she had shared way too much.

But now was not the time to reflect on indiscretions she could not change—today she needed to battle panic and sit herself in a kayak, to ensure the teens had a brilliant day and to maximise exposure for the foundation.

She took one last look at her reflection. Walking boots, suitable kayaking clothes, minimal waterproof make-up, hair carefully pulled back in a seemingly causal ponytail. She was good to go.

A knock on the door heralded Daniel, and she forced a smile to her lips.

A smile he paid no heed to. 'It's not too late to back out.'

'No.'

Focusing on keeping her expression neutral, all signs of nerves carefully locked away, she walked alongside him to the car, climbed in and concentrated on deep breathing and meditative thoughts until they arrived at their destination.

Before the ordeal of the water she had to face—and charm—the barrage of press cameramen.

'Hi, guys. Good to see you all here.'

Friendly smile in place. *Tick*. Stance relaxed. *Tick*. Showing no untoward awareness of Daniel. *God, she hoped so.*

'I hope my team made it clear that today is about the Caversham Foundation. More than that, it is about the kids who are here to learn a new skill in this beautiful place.'

'Aw, come on, Kaitlin. Can't we ask a few questions about you?'

Kaitlin tipped her head to one side as if in consideration, as if she hadn't anticipated the request. 'Two personal questions—as long as I have your promise that your coverage will focus on what is most important here. And that's *not* me.'

'Deal.'

'Then go ahead.'

'Have you heard from Prince Frederick?'

'That one is nice and easy. No, I haven't.' For a moment disquiet touched her; they had agreed to keep in touch, to co-ordinate publicity. She'd kept her side—had emailed him a schedule of her plans—but there had been no word from the Prince.

'Are you feeling any regrets?' came the next question.

'No. Of course it's sad when a relationship doesn't work out, but I feel confident that we made the right decision for us right now.' Irritation touched her—those words left the whole thing open, and she knew it—it seemed as though she was following her parents' dictum on automatic. 'And I am focused on moving on with my life.'

'Right.' Daniel stepped in. 'The two questions are over and now Lady Kaitlin will demonstrate her kayaking skills.'

It would be fine.

As long as she didn't think about the water. Better to focus on the existence of the tandem kayak—on Daniel's aura, his reassurance and his strength. Those images crushed the slithering doubt, propelled her forward to the group of teenagers who stood in a suspicious huddle by the waterside.

A couple looked enthused, but the majority looked sullen, despite the efforts of the woman who accompanied them to chivvy them along.

Empathy stirred—memories of being told to pose, to smile, to act like a Lady when inside she had felt shrivelled and unclean after the kidnap.

Maybe these kids didn't feel like smiling—maybe being a recipient of charity didn't always inspire gratitude. Maybe they felt out of their depth, thrust into doing an activity they didn't want to do with Lady Kaitlin Derwent—a woman they probably despised as being a stuck-up, upper-class snob.

'Hey, guys. I'm Kaitlin, and this is only the second time I have kayaked in my life. I have never been an outdoor person—I'm a city girl through and through—and I sympathise if you don't actually want to be here. I had some serious doubts too, and as Daniel will attest when I kayaked for the first time yesterday I capsized. If you're lucky it may happen again.'

A few tentative smiles, and even though she was well aware they were more laughing *at* her than *with* her it was still a step in the right direction.

'The *good* thing, though, was that I was wearing a lifejacket—and whilst I am aware it won't be winning any fashion awards, I was glad of it. So everyone please buckle up.'

Cue a few groans.

Then one boy who had been glaring at her said, 'So you don't kayak and you don't like the outdoors. Whatcha doing here, then? Come to lord it over us poor little delinquents so you can feel good about yourself?'

'No.' Kaitlin stepped forward so she was near enough for him to sense her sincerity but not so close that his space was invaded. 'I was born into the family I was born into, just like you were born into the family *you* were born into. That's the lottery of life. But it doesn't give me the right to "lord it" over anyone, delinquent or not. Just like *your* family background, whatever that may be, doesn't give you the right to *be* a delinquent.

I'm here because, rightly or wrongly, my presence here does get publicity—and I think you deserve a share of that publicity. At the end of the day if you wish to talk directly to the reporters you can. And feel free to give your honest opinion on the day and me.'

Even as she said the words she knew the offer was nuts—a publicity gamble of the most stupid kind. But she didn't care. It had felt…right. Even if her parents would condemn it as foolish beyond belief.

With one last smile she turned and walked back to Daniel, who was eying her with curiosity and more than a hint of admiration, as well a touch of surprise.

'Lady Kaitlin in action. They all look a lot more enthused than they did a few minutes ago, and that boy is definitely less hostile.'

'I told you: I do the research, I do the groundwork—I agreed to do this and I'll do it to the best of my ability.'

'It's more than that. You didn't need research to achieve what you just did—that was *you*, Kaitlin, not your preparation, faultless thought that was.'

'Thank you.' Absurdly, warmth encased her at his approval, sufficient to embolden her as she stared into the depths of the canal. 'Let's kayak.'

Two days later

Kaitlin ached, but it was a good ache—the kind of ache that spoke of outdoor exercise, clean air, mountains and glens.

A twinge of nerves was accompanied by more than a hint of anticipation as she hesitated outside the lounge door. The past two nights she had scurried to her room with a take-out sandwich, needing time alone to erase the Daniel effect. It was ridiculous, given her genuine absorption in the activities and the teens, and yet the whole time her body had hummed with a constant awareness—one she knew mirrored his own. She'd sensed it in the way his eyes rested on her, felt the tension vibrate from him when they were close together.

So the obvious answer was not to get close.

But right now she had no choice—there was no way round the need to actually speak with him face to face.

Get on with it, Kaitlin.

She pushed the door open and entered, swallowed the catch of breath that afflicted her whenever she saw him. Sitting on the sofa, intent on his laptop, he looked so...*yummy.* Dark hair shower-damp, dressed in a white T-shirt that showed the honey tone of his skin, the muscular forearms with a smattering of hair.

He turned to look at her, and heat lit his blue eyes for a scant second.

'Hi. Sorry—I didn't mean to disturb you.'

'It's fine.' He pushed the screen away from him and rubbed a hand over his face. 'What can I do for you?'

'I...I wondered if I could talk to you about something?'

'Sure. Would you like a drink? You definitely deserve one—you've done a brilliant job the past two days.'

The words were warm, yet the tone didn't match—there was a near cynicism that confused her. 'You sound surprised. Or upset?'

A frown creased his forehead as he rose and walked to the sideboard, where he opened a bottle of red wine. Turning, he shrugged. 'Not at all.

As you said, you had a job to do and you have executed it perfectly. The press have loved this aspect of Lady Kaitlin. So have the teenagers.'

Again, despite the positive words she sensed an undercurrent.

'I sense a reservation.'

He hesitated, and then tipped his palms in the air. 'I don't get it. Is it real or a gigantic PR exercise to you? You seem so natural with the teenagers, and I can't tell if you mean it or if you are simply furthering your image.' He poured the wine into two glasses. 'Not that it matters.'

Anger and hurt swirled together in her stomach. 'Excuse me? You think I'm *faking* this?'

'That's it. I don't know. *You* are the one who told me image is everything.'

The words halted her—she *had* said that, and when she had agreed to do this her motivation had been to introduce a new facet of Lady Kaitlin Derwent. Accepting the glass he handed her, she looked down into the ruby liquid and thought back over the past days. Looked back up at him.

'These past days haven't been about my image. It's been about *them*.' Tom and Celia and Liz and Darren and…and all the youngsters she'd spoken with. 'Some of what they have been through makes my blood run cold. I like every one of them and I want to help them. For real—not as part of a PR exercise for me.'

She broke off at the sudden smile that turned up his lips and made her tummy flip. 'What?'

'That's the first time you've sounded so passionate about something.'

'I *do* feel passionate about it. Until now most of my charitable efforts have been attending events or fundraising for Derwent Manor. This is different. I've never felt so *involved*. I care about these kids.' She glanced at him and the knowledge of a shared belief made warmth bubble inside her. 'I think you do too.'

Because she'd seen him—the way he spoke with them, the discussions he'd had with them— she'd seen how serious some of them had been. Had also seen his patience as he explained how to do something, the way he'd genuinely listened to them, bantered, joked…as if he felt a connection.

'I do.'

'Why?' Kaitlin hadn't meant to ask the question but she wanted to know.

'Why do *you*?' he countered.

'Because they have made me realise how lucky I am—made me see how petty my own concerns are.' Even the horror of her kidnap faded into insignificance against what some of the children had had to face in their short lifespans. 'They've made me...*feel*.' The admission was almost too much, though it was true—these kids had got under her skin. 'Feel as if I want to help,' she completed hurriedly. 'Now your turn.'

'It's as you said. For years I have spent every minute of the day focused on success. *My* success. These past days I've wanted to help *them*.'

They stared at each other—the shared revelation buzzed between them, created a connection that shimmered in the air.

Kaitlin took a gulp of wine, felt the spice and berry notes tingle on her tongue as she tried to pull her shattered senses into order. 'Which brings me to my idea.'

'Go ahead. But sit down first.'

She sank down onto the cream armchair and tucked her feet under her. 'I know the outdoors is important, and how much benefit the kids have reaped from the kayaking and the hiking. But I want to do something a bit different tomorrow.'

'You don't have to do anything tomorrow. You've done your bit.'

'I know, but I want to—and I believe I've come up with something useful. Most of those children don't want charity—they want to make it on their own. The problem is the odds are stacked against them from the get-go. They will be judged because of their backgrounds and if they get knocked back time and again they will give up. I want to increase the odds of their success. I want to teach them how to project confidence even when they don't feel it inside, to wear the right clothes, walk the right walk.' All the things *she* had painstakingly done to construct Lady Kaitlin Derwent. 'That will give them an edge.'

'Is that how you feel? No confidence on the inside?'

His voice was low, genuine, and the edges of her façade crumbled.

'Of course not.' The words sounded brittle, even to her own ears. She uncurled her feet, placed the wine glass down with a *thunk* and rose to her feet. 'Anyway, this isn't about me. The point is I'd like to do this. I'll take them shopping—you don't need designer outfits or lots of money, it's getting the colours right, a suitable cut, finding a style. I can help them—I know I can. So what do you think?'

'I think it's a fantastic idea.'

'You do?'

'I do.'

Kaitlin felt her lips curve up in a completely spontaneous smile. 'Fabulous.' She took a step forward, towards him. 'Thank you, Daniel.' Reaching out, she put a hand on his arm.

Big mistake, Kaitlin.

She'd swear she'd heard a fizz as her fingers contacted with his skin. Worse, she might well have given the smallest of moans.

Move your hand.

But her brain refused to send the requisite signal. Instead her gaze remained riveted to her hand on his arm.

'Kaitlin...'

His voice was ever so slightly strained and she looked up, saw the unmistakeable heat in his eyes and felt an answering thrill.

'I...'

'Dammit.'

With that he put his hand on her waist and gently tugged her forward into his embrace.

Desire knocked common sense down and trampled it; her arms reached up and looped round his neck. And then his lips touched hers and she was lost.

The taste of wine, the clean, just-out-of-the-shower scent of him, the intensity as he deepened the kiss all spiralled inside her. Thought was impossible. Ripples of desire tugged her nerve-endings and the intensity of sensation hollowed her tummy, caused a deep yearning for more. Pressing herself against him, she revelled in the strength of his body, in his small groan as she parted her lips.

She never wanted the moment to end—but finally common sense picked itself off the floor and shrieked a message, jolted her back to reality.

Pulling back, she stared at him—then away. Caught an image of herself in the ornate gilt mirror above the mantel. *Hell*. She barely recognised herself. Flushed, lips swollen, hair dishevelled, eyes glazed. What was she *doing*?

Focus—she had to pull this together. Had to locate her true self, pull the Lady Kaitlin Derwent mantle round her.

'I'm sorry. That was obviously not a good move for either of us.'

Amazing how she could keep her voice so light. A quick smooth of her hair, a step backwards and an aloof, self-deprecating smile.

'I think the wine must have gone to my head on top of all that unaccustomed exercise. The best thing is to forget all about it and put it behind us.'

His blue eyes bored into her. 'If that's what you want.'

Her heart pounded her ribcage. 'There isn't any alternative.'

'Sure there is. There is always a choice, Kaitlin. We could take this further. Instead of fighting this attraction we could enjoy it. Enjoy Venice together.'

Temptation crooked a finger and Kaitlin dug her nails into her palms. *At least think about it*, wailed her inner voice, but this time Kaitlin was prepared, and common sense was ready and waiting.

'The risk is too great. All it takes is for one reporter to suspect. Hell, we could have been photographed through the window just now. And I won't risk the scandal for the sake of a few hours in bed.'

Her parents would be livid, the press would have a field-day and she would have regrets—because it wasn't Lady Kaitlin Derwent's style.

'So from now on it is business all the way. I'll see you in the morning.'

CHAPTER NINE

DANIEL LOOKED ACROSS the private jet to where Kaitlin sat, back ramrod-straight, not so much as a crease in her white and blue floral dress, her focus apparently completely on the book in her hand. No sign now of the Kaitlin of two days before, curled up on the sofa, relaxed and animated, as she talked about her plans for the teens.

That Kaitlin had gone for good after the kiss they had shared—a kiss that still haunted his body and his mind. Despite the common sense that told him he had been a fool one hundred times over to suggest a fling with Kaitlin. Kaitlin was too complex, too different from the women he usually slept with.

Plus, the idea was fraught with risks of disastrous consequences for either or both of them. Three days with Kaitlin wasn't worth the risk of having his family unearthed. Three days with him wasn't worth Kaitlin scuppering her chances of a reunion with Prince Frederick or an alliance with some other member of royalty.

That was what she wanted—the path she had chosen or had had chosen for her—a life of wealth and security and pomp and ceremony and children. He could offer her only the first, on a temporary basis—hardly an offer worth consideration. And an offer he should never had considered.

He must have been mad to so much as kiss her.

Since then she had been coolly polite, kept herself distant both physically and mentally, and they hadn't exchanged a word in private, hadn't spent more than a minute alone. But, hell, he had a captive audience now, at forty thousand feet in the air—there was nowhere for her to go and his inner devil prompted him to speak.

'Good book?' he enquired.

'Very, thank you.'

'Hmm… Because I can't help but notice you haven't turned a page in the past twenty minutes.'

Her lips pressed together in clear annoyance. 'You must be mistaken.'

'I don't think so. You do realise that even though we have decided not to pursue our attraction further that doesn't mean we have to give up on actual conversation?'

'Conversation is overrated.' Kaitlin shook her head. 'Sorry—that was rude. But it was conversation that led us to being so stupid, so it seems to me that we should keep all contact to a minimum.'

'I don't think that will work.

'Why?'

'Because I figure we need to talk about what happened and this seems like a good opportunity.'

'There is nothing to say.'

'So you still want to try and pretend it didn't happen?'

'Yup.'

'Make like that kiss was imaginary?'

'Yup.'

'Not going to work. You don't want the press or anyone to suspect a connection between us— but ignoring our attraction will make our body language awkward and we'll pitch a vibe someone like April Fotherington will pick up. We have a press conference scheduled before the ball. And after.'

'So what's your solution?'

'We spend as much time together as possible and eradicate the awkwardness.'

He could almost see another negative trembling on her lips, and then she closed her eyes and muttered something under her breath. Something that sounded like, 'Lady Kaitlin, do your stuff.'

Opening her eyes, she looked at him coolly. 'Fair enough. We'll give that a try. Let's start now and discuss the plan for Venice.' Leaning down, she pulled out the ubiquitous notebook. 'I've already looked at all the auction items and done some research. I've also studied the guest list and identified any people I know—art gallery owners or family friends—so I'll make sure I network with them, raise awareness so that people will dig deep at the auction. I'll also see if I can persuade a few more donations out of people as surprise items for the auction.'

'Sounds like you have it covered. Just like you had it covered with the kids. You've been so busy hiding out in your room I haven't had a chance to tell you how impressed I was. Your workshop was amazing.'

Kaitlin had taken the youngsters shopping, given each one of them a one-on-one tutorial on style and budget, followed by a workshop on image projection. There had been gales of laughter, and at the end of it they had all looked like new people. He'd been left in no doubt that any preconceptions about aristocracy had been knocked to flinders.

'Enough so that I want to talk to Ethan and Ruby about you running those workshops regularly, if you would be up for it.'

'Really?'

For a moment her face lit up and he blinked at the sheer beauty of her.

'Really. What do you think?'

Suddenly, like the Christmas tree lights being extinguished on Twelfth Night, her expression was closed off. 'It may be too big a commitment. I guess the workshops would be all over the country, and it would be hard for me to juggle them. Maybe I could train someone else to do them?'

Daniel frowned 'Or maybe you could throw

in the art gallery job and build up a whole new business? People would pay to learn how to project confidence. You have the organisational skills needed, and the business acumen, and...'

A firm shake of her head greeted this suggestion. Firm enough that her gorgeous hair rippled. 'I'm happy where I am now. I don't want to stray out of my comfort zone. I know where I am with the art gallery and I like that.'

Daniel frowned, wondered why Kaitlin had set her comfort zone at such a low threshold. Something didn't add up, but the rigidity of her expression indicated that she wouldn't be offering him the solution to the sum.

Her head bent over the notebook. 'Ethan seems to have been a bit vague about exactly what he needs us to do prior to the ball.'

'Make sure all the arrangements are in place—check the catering, ensure all the auction items have been collected and stored. With luck we'll have some time to explore Venice. Have you been before?'

'No.' Her expression was neutral, with no hint of anticipation at visiting one of the most historic, beautiful cities in the world. 'Have you?'

'Yes. Once.'

His mother had always wanted to go to Venice—had told him how his father and she had dreamed of one day settling in the city where his father's people had originated. Daniel had promised her that one day he would take her. Instead he had gone on his own, in celebration when he'd graduated from law school. He had wandered the narrow streets and determination had pulsed in his veins that he *would* succeed and one day he *would* bring his mother to the city.

Now, eight years later, he was no longer so sure and loss touched him.

Seeing her eyes rest on his face with question and concern, he smiled. 'It's an incredible place.'

'I am quite happy to field the organisational side of the ball to give you time to see Venice,' she offered.

'Absolutely not. We've agreed that the more time we spend together the better.' An arrangement that suddenly seemed foolhardy. 'So we'll organise together and explore together.'

A definite wince greeted his suggestion, but before he could comment the pilot announced their descent to Marco Polo airport and he figured it was better to leave well enough alone.

As Kaitlin emerged from the jet onto the Tarmac she could feel the onset of panic start to unfurl in her tummy, despite her efforts to prepare. Airports always had the ability to overwhelm her—too dangerous, insecure, too busy.

Instinct had her stepping her towards Daniel. *Bad idea.*

The memory of their kiss seared her with a burn that increased the closer he was. Which, perversely, was the reason for her agreement to spend time with him. For the first time in over a decade Kaitlin was not in control of an emotion and, dammit, she *loathed* that sensation. So she *would* learn to subdue this unwanted attraction. Just as she had subdued panic, anger, anxiety… *insert emotion here.*

Once they'd negotiated Customs a man bustled towards them, a beaming smile on his face. 'Signor Harrington and Signora Derwent. I am Roberto, and I am delighted to welcome you on behalf of the hotel. But first—the press have contacted us, requesting to see you on your arrival. Of course if you do not wish it we will ensure your arrival is kept private...'

Kaitlin kept her expression neutral, though her brain whirred furiously. There had been no scheduled press meeting, yet they couldn't forego a chance of extra publicity for the ball.

Daniel had clearly come to the same conclusion. 'We'll do a brief meet-and-greet.'

'Very well. Now, come with me, for I have arranged for you to travel to the hotel by water taxi. We have our own private jetty at the *palazzo*.'

Just what she needed. But no way could she disappoint Roberto's expectant smile. 'That sounds wonderful, *signor*—you have my utmost thanks.'

Within minutes Roberto had driven them to a boathouse, where they boarded a polished wood-panelled boat. Averting her eyes from the water, Kaitlin climbed in, aware of Daniel's watchful gaze.

'Have a wonderful journey. I will meet you at the hotel.'

Once Roberto had gone, Daniel questioned

her. 'Is this a problem? There *are* other ways of getting to the hotel.'

'I know that.' Ferry, bus, train… She'd researched them all. 'But it would have been rude and provoked questions to refuse this. Anyway, I'll be fine—it's not as if I can fall in.'

Kaitlin perched on the cream leather seat and watched as Daniel settled opposite her. Those blue eyes held a hint of scepticism and she forced herself to lean back, though nothing could have compelled her to actually look out of the window as the boat set off.

To her relief Daniel maintained a flow of conversation, including a potted history of Venice, so all she had to do was listen.

As she focused on his voice and concentrated on memorising the facts she felt better. Perhaps more than anything his sheer presence helped—the solid, reassuring strength of him. Which didn't make sense. The Prince had never made her feel like this. Even Gabe, her big brother, didn't have this effect on her.

Ugh. Gritting her teeth, Kaitlin shifted ever so slightly away from him. Her treacherous body could not be so foolish as to trust in Daniel Harrington—a man she would never see again after this trip to Venice. Though perhaps in that case she might as well make use of him whilst she could—after all, the most important imperative was to get through this ride.

Eventually they neared their destination and she began to prepare for the press conference. The water taxi glided between the bright mooring poles that demarcated the hotel's boat deck and she braced herself for the bevy of reporters standing on the wooden slats.

As she alighted her relief at feeling dry land underfoot was matched by trepidation as her finely honed publicity antennae tuned into an undercurrent. These reporters had an anticipatory air about them—which could only mean one thing.

'They've got something,' she murmured to Daniel as foreboding tickled her nerves.

Surely no one could have glimpsed that kiss?

'So, Kaitlin, can you shed any light on why Prince Frederick has made an unannounced trip to India?'

Careful.

Her brain clicked and whirred, joined the dots

and anticipated the next volley even as her lips turned up in the trademark Kaitlin smile.

'No, that's news to me as well.'

'Do you think there could be a link to Sunita?'

The model and Bollywood actress known only as Sunita *had* been linked to Frederick, but as far as Kaitlin knew she had been one of Frederick's many short-term liaisons with beautiful women, with nothing in particular to distinguish her from any other.

'I really couldn't comment on that.'

'So there is no connection to your break-up?'

'No.'

'Perhaps the best person to ask that question of would be Sunita. Or even the Prince himself.'

Daniel's interruption turned the attention to him and April Fotherington stepped forward, her eyes darting from Daniel to Kaitlin with curiosity.

'Perhaps you're right. So let's discuss the past few days. How was your stay in that lovely cottage on the Caledonian Canal? I heard it was quite cosy.'

It was a shot in the dark—Kaitlin *knew* that— yet she also knew she had given the smallest of tell-tale flinches. Dammit—Daniel had been right. They needed to eradicate whatever signals of awkwardness they exuded.

'I'd hardly describe a three-bedroom property, however picturesque, as "cosy".' Daniel's voice held exactly the right mix of amusement and derision. 'I know you all want to sell copy, and I get it that that means you want to believe there is an angle here, but there isn't. Kaitlin and I want this week to be about the Caversham Foundation—so if you want a different type of story then I repeat: go and find Prince Frederick and Sunita and try your luck there.'

Outrage swirled inside Kaitlin at the realisation that he'd thrown Frederick to the wolves even as she acknowledged that it appeared to have worked. The reporters had turned their questions to the upcoming ball. So, smile in place, she answered questions about the guest list, her outfit and her shoes, all the time aware that April in particular was watching her with speculation.

Once the press had dispersed they made their way into the sanctuary of the hotel—where Kaitlin stopped short at the sight of the lobby's sheer elegant magnificence. The pink and white chequered floor, the marble busts that lined the walls and the enormous lantern that dominated the ceiling all combined to create an opulence that inspired awe.

Two hotel staff glided towards them, one bearing a tray with two flutes of sparkling amber liquid. 'To refresh you after the journey,' one murmured.

Within seconds, almost without knowing how it had happened, she and Daniel were seated on chairs of extraordinary comfort and Roberto had materialised in front of them.

'Welcome. Your suite is of course ready—two en-suite double bedrooms, with a sitting room in between for you to work. I hope that is acceptable—we accommodated Signora Derwent at late notice.'

'That sounds wonderful,' Kaitlin lied as she stemmed a panic of a different type. A suite sounded too...*close.*

For heaven's sake.

They would be separated by a lounge, and she knew that the rooms in this hotel were positively palatial. Yet a quick sideways glance at Daniel showed a definite tension to his jaw—hard to figure whether that should make her feel better or worse.

'I will take you up, and on the way I will give you a brief tour,' Roberto continued, pride clear in his voice. 'The hotel is truly worthy of a grand tour. It was built in the sixteenth century as a *palazzo* and we have changed as little as possible of its splendour—whilst of course incorporating maximum twenty-first-century comfort and amenities.'

As they followed Roberto to the grand sweeping curve of the staircase and through a maze of passageways and public rooms it seemed clear that he hadn't exaggerated. The restoration was a timeless fusion of old and new, the colour schemes a tribute to taste. Historic murals and frescoes were subtly showcased, the library felt heavy with knowledge, and yet the overall impression was one of elegant, gorgeous comfort.

Then they came to their suite, and Roberto stopped at the door and handed them two ornate iron keys. 'One last item—we have arranged complimentary tickets for a private tour of the Doge's Palace today. Tomorrow we will meet to show you all the arrangements for the ball.' A small bow and he turned and headed back to the staircase.

For a moment they both stood in the panelled passageway and eyed the door, before Daniel swiped a hand down his face and stepped forward. 'Shall we?'

She followed him through and her eyes widened as she looked around the lounge. 'Wow!'

But Daniel didn't seem inclined to view the authentic silk wall coverings, or to *ooh* and *ah* over the sixteenth-century architecture, or even the intricate splendour of the chandelier.

Instead he leant back against the wall and surveyed her. 'Is it likely that Prince Frederick is with Sunita?'

'I don't know.'

'Don't you care?'

The thought caused a mix of emotions. The sensation of a weight lifted from her shoulders, alongside a ripple of fear of the unknown... 'If you mean am I hurt or jealous? Then, no, I'm not.'

A lightning-fast thought shot through her head—an image of Daniel with a woman—and to her surprise her hands clenched involuntarily. Of *course* that wasn't what Daniel meant—he wouldn't be interested in her emotional state.

Time to retrieve the gaffe.

'In terms of how the publicity will affect the ball—I don't know. I don't think the press will lose interest in me, but you're right. It depends on whether the story is true. Either way I think it's win-win for us. If he is with Sunita they will still want my reaction. If he isn't we haven't lost anything. Right now I'm more concerned about April Fotherington. So let's hope you're right— the more time we spend together the less awkward our body language will become.'

Though now she came to think about it that didn't make a vast amount of sense. But no matter—there was no choice.

She glanced at her watch. 'Anyway, I'm going to unpack and settle in before the Doge's Palace tour.'

Once in her room Kaitlin sat on the edge of her sumptuous king-sized bed and took a moment to appreciate the room's baroque splendour. Gold and gilt and intricate plasterwork was offset by the minimalist functional furniture, the heavy curtains that would guarantee a good night's sleep.

For a moment she was tempted to lie back and simply study the ceiling, adorned with the beauty of a painting by one of Venice's best-known artists centuries before. To shut herself in this sanctuary of a room—away from the tumultuous feelings Daniel evoked, away from the panic it was becoming harder to keep at bay—and admit it was all too much. That she'd bitten off more than she could fit in her mouth, let alone chew.

No! That was *not* her way. So instead, with resolution, she walked to the window and looked out—perhaps if she looked around from the safety of her room she could at least acclimatise herself?

But seconds later she propelled herself backwards, her senses reeling as panic slammed her. Unfamiliarity surrounded her—but, worse, everywhere she looked there was *water*.

Tendrils of memory unfurled and clamped her in a stranglehold of panic. The rough, grating tone of the kidnappers, the heart wrenching terror, the conviction that they would drown her. The blindfold…their chilling description of exactly what would happen to her as she drowned… The humiliation of her own voice begging, promising to do as they said.

Not now. These memories could not resurface now.

She backed further away from the window, hauled in a breath and perched on the end of the bed. She closed her eyes and tried to call up peaceful, safe thoughts.

'Kaitlin?'

Daniel's deep voice pervaded her meditation and she opened her eyes.

'I knocked three times. I was worried. Are you ready to go?'

Realisation hit her that she couldn't do it; she'd shot her bolt, thrown in the towel—you name it, she'd done it.

'Actually, I'm exhausted. I think I'll give it a miss.' Rising to her feet she tried to project cool assurance.

'"*Give it a miss*"? A private tour round the Doge's Palace your first time in Venice?' His voice registered utter disbelief. 'Are you nuts?'

'No. It's been a tiring few days, and I want to

conserve my energy for the ball and the preparations.' Turning, she shook her hair slightly forward. 'But you go.'

A frown, and then he shrugged. 'OK. But I think you're making a mistake. The Doge's Palace epitomises Venice at the height of its power—every single one of Venice's greatest painters and sculptors is represented somewhere. That palace is where history was made.'

A solitary tear prickled at her eyelid—damn it, she *wanted* to go. Wanted to experience Venice, see the splendour of what he described with such fervour. But how could she risk being overtaken by panic in the cobbled streets? Or even in the immensity of the palace itself? And panic was imminent—she sensed it.

'You go,' she repeated.

CHAPTER TEN

DANIEL REACHED THE door of the suite, opened it and exited into the corridor. If Kaitlin truly wanted to pass up this opportunity then that was her choice. That was what he believed in—the power of choice. Yet her decision stung more than it should.

Don't make this personal.

Because his lawyer's instinct told him that Kaitlin had withheld information. Impossible that the woman who had embraced the Highlands, who worked in an art gallery, wouldn't want to go to the Doge's Palace.

Not his business.

Yes, it was.

He turned round and retraced his steps, re-entered the suite and banged a perfunctory knock on her bedroom door.

A few seconds later Kaitlin peered out and

surprise widened her green eyes. 'Did you forget something?'

'Yes, I did. I forgot you.'

'Huh?'

'You need to come to the palace. Think how it will look to Roberto, to the guests at the ball, when they hear you passed up this chance. If it's because you don't want my company I'd rather you went and I stayed here—I've seen the palace before.'

'It's fine, Daniel. I told you to go.'

'Nope.' Daniel sat down in an armchair and stretched his legs out.

'What are you doing now?'

'Sitting.'

'Why?'

'Because I'm not going to the Doge's Palace unless you come with me or explain why you won't.'

Her mouth formed a small circle of outrage. 'That is ridiculous. It's daft for us both to miss out.'

A frown creased her forehead as she realised the impact of her words.

'So you admit you're missing out?'

'Stop it!'

'Not till you explain.'

Indecision etched her face and her hands smoothed the skirt of her dress, her fingers outlining first one printed blue flower then another, and then she shook her head. 'It doesn't matter.'

'Yes, it does.'

And it did. As he looked at her he could see hurt in the strain that lined the green of her eyes and the uncharacteristic slump to her posture.

'Tell me.'

'Leave it, Daniel. It's not important.'

'It is to me.'

'Why?' The syllable was tart, almost a challenge. 'If you're worried that it will impact the ball, it won't. I'll come up with a plausible reason.'

'I don't care about the ball. I care about—'

You? No.

'I care about the fact that a colleague of mine will miss out on an opportunity to experience something wonderful. Plus, I believe that you *want* to go. So what's stopping you?'

'It's personal, and you and I don't do personal.'

Of course he knew he should leave it, but he

couldn't—the knowledge that he was near to an important truth was something he couldn't ignore or impede.

'Maybe we should change that.'

She shook her head, and a short, mirthless laugh dropped from her lips. 'By which you mean *I* should share something personal with *you*, not vice versa.'

The truth caused heat to warm the back of his neck. *Touché*. Now he really needed to back off. But the glint in her eye, the challenge, brought out the advocate in him.

'I can do personal. I just choose not to. You don't do personal because you don't trust anyone. You think if you confide in me I may use the information—go public, tell the reporters… I won't. You have already trusted me with Barcelona—why not go a step further?'

'Why does it matter to you?'

'Because I want you to see the Doge's Palace.' *Keep it casual*.

'And you think that if I confide in you the issue will go away?'

'It's worth a shot.'

A long silence and then, 'It won't, but you're

right. You already have so much power over me, one more item is neither here nor there.' Hands in her lap, she took in an audible breath before saying, 'I suffer from panic attacks.'

The words took a couple of seconds to register—given the serenity and calm for which Kaitlin was famed, they seemed incredible. But then he remembered Barcelona—his first glimpse of 'Lynette'—remembered Kaitlin's frenzy when she'd fallen into the water, her over-the-top preparations for Scotland and Venice. Admiration touched him at her courage in taking on both places.

'I'm so sorry, Kaitlin. I wish I could say more, but it makes everything you have achieved even more impressive.' He rose to his feet, squashed the urge to go and sit next to her, put an arm around her and tell her he'd make it all OK, and started to pace instead. 'I'm guessing water and new places trigger the attacks?'

'*Anything* can trigger the attacks.' There was bitterness and resignation in her tone. 'But, yes, I find unfamiliar places overwhelming—and as for water... I do my best to avoid it.'

'Is that what you've been advised to do? Avoid

anything that might trigger the panic?' He was no expert, but that tactic would surely impose nigh on impossible limitations.

'It's what I've worked out for myself.'

There was defiance in the jut of her chin and defence in the folding of her arms as she glared at him in a clear dare to challenge her.

It was a dare he was more than happy to take up. 'How long have you had these attacks?'

'Since childhood.'

'Then surely you must have seen a doctor or a counsellor? Someone must have noticed you panic—your parents, a teacher, Gabe, Cora...'

'I didn't need to see anyone.'

'Did your parents know?'

Easy, Daniel. This isn't a witness in the stand.

'Yes. But they decided it was better to deal with it ourselves.'

By that, Daniel was pretty sure Kaitlin meant they had left her to deal with it by herself. His mind whirred, put together the hints and conversational snippets of the past few days.

'Something happened to incite the panic and they didn't want the publicity.'

'Leave it.'

Her face had blanched and Daniel knew that whatever had happened to her had been catastrophic.

'I'm not under oath and I will not discuss the cause of the attacks.'

There was strength and dignity in her stance and in her voice, underlain with such vulnerability that his chest ached. Whatever burden she bore she clearly carried it alone. Anger with her parents caused his stride to increase even as he determined not to spook her further.

'I understand. I won't ask any more. But I strongly believe that you need to talk to an expert.'

'I have it under control.'

'I totally admire that you have managed this for so long, but there may be a better way. A way to overcome the panic rather than control it—a way to make it go away. The best way to find out is to talk to someone—an expert, a therapist.'

'I can't do that.'

'Yes, you can. If the story leaks out so be it.' Halting in front of her, he reached out a hand and pulled her up, kept her hand in his. 'Kaitlin, this is your *life* we're talking about.'

'Stop it. You're messing with my head. My life is fine as it is.'

'Yes, it is. I would never belittle what you have achieved. But the panic imposes limits on you. Without it your life could take a different trajectory.'

'That is akin to the assertion that a blind person's life would be different if they could see. It is as it is.'

'Maybe it doesn't have to be. You owe it to yourself to find out.'

She huffed out a sigh that signalled exasperation, pulled her hand from his. 'Until you came along my life was on the exact trajectory I wanted it to be on, and I have every intention of returning it there after Venice. End of discussion.'

Frustrated, he opened his mouth to continue the argument—until he saw the stubborn set to her jaw. Perhaps a softly-softly approach would make more sense, but he wouldn't let this go for long. Just for now.

'Fair enough. No more discussion. But I have an idea about the Doge's Palace. Think back to Barcelona.'

'I really don't want to remember Barcelona.'

'Yes, you do.' He took her hands back, ignored the shiver of sensation that rippled up his arm in response. 'You walked the streets, you went into the hustle and bustle of a tapas bar and you were fine.'

'That's because—'

She broke off, pressed her lips together, and he wondered what she had been about to say.

'Because you were 'Lynette'?'

'Something like that. But that won't work here.'

'No. But you have something else here that you had in Barcelona.'

Her eyes narrowed.

'Me,' he completed.

'You?' Disbelief tinged the very air. 'So you reckon *you* are the magical solution to my panic attacks?'

'No. Of course not. But maybe I can be a temporary sticking plaster. I promise that I will keep you safe. If you can bring yourself to believe that, maybe it will help keep the panic at bay enough to allow you to appreciate Venice. I promise you that if it all gets too much I will get you back here quickly and discreetly, and although I understand there is nothing tangible you are worried about I am more than equipped to keep you safe from pickpockets. What do you think?'

Kaitlin moved away from his presence and walked over to the window, almost as if to brave the view of the scenery again.

'Why does this matter to you? Why not just leave me here and go and enjoy Venice?'

'Because that would make me a complete heel. And I could use the company.'

Seeing the disbelief in her face, he dug deep. Kaitlin had shared something huge with him. Surely he could choose to reciprocate a little.

'It's the truth. My father died before I was born. But my mother told me that they had planned to move to Venice some day. So the city always makes me feel a little melancholy.'

Kaitlin's eyes darted to his face. 'That must be hard—never having known your dad.'

'I had my mother, and she was amazing.'

'She must have felt so blessed to have had you.'

Blessed. Daniel didn't think so. Oh, his mother had loved him—so much that she had sacrificed her very soul for him. It was a shame it had proved such a poor investment. The bitter taste of guilt flooded him and he swiped a hand down his face. *Enough.* This was about Kaitlin.

She looked at him, her green eyes serious.

'OK. Let's do this. Doge's Palace, here I come.'

As they approached the splendour of the palace Kaitlin caught her breath in sheer awe. Here she was, standing in front of this incredible building, and a wave of emotion swathed her—a lightness, an unfamiliar joy that made her want to laugh out loud.

Without thought she reached out, took Daniel's hand and smiled up at him. 'This is fabulous— thank you for your persistence.'

'No trouble.'

But it had been—Daniel had cared enough to return for her, to convince her to accompany him, and the idea sent further warmth to her insides.

Careful, Kaitlin.

But she didn't want to be careful; for once she wanted to go with the flow, with the thoroughly unfamiliar sense of trust.

Bad idea.

But it wasn't. It wasn't as if she proposed to trust in Daniel long-term. This was purely a three-day fix. If he could help her enjoy Venice then it made sense to let him. And his presence did seem to have a positive effect on her panic—sure, the swirl of unease was present, but it hadn't escalated.

Now they stood in the slanting Venetian spring sunshine and gazed at the Gothic structure of the enormous building—an epicentre of history where political decisions had been made, where justice had been meted out over the centuries by each elected Doge.

'It is such an influential place, and yet it has a fairytale element.'

Enhanced by the candy cane effect of huge walls of white limestone and pink marble and the series of balconies.

Daniel nodded. 'Apparently experts say that the sense of lightness is because of the way it was built, with the loggias below and the solid walls above. That gives it an openness that was meant to indicate how powerful Venice was.

Most cities back then would build more forti-
fied castles.'

Suddenly aware that she was still holding
Daniel's hand, she looked down at their clasped
fingers and wondered what to do. Placing temporary trust in him was one thing—venturing
into any realm of physical contact was another.
Yet letting go required an effort of will that had
her alarm bells ringing again.

'Shall we go in?'

Daniel nodded and they made their way into
the courtyard.

'It's impossible to know what to look at first,'
Kaitlin marvelled.

'Yes.'

She glanced at him, observed the light in his
blue eyes as they rested on her, and felt heat
climb her cheekbones. Suddenly their surroundings, despite the magnificence of the giant cer-
emonial staircase, the enormous statues of
Neptune and Mars, even the imposing yet ethe-
real beauty of the Foscari arch, faded into the
background.

All she could see—all she was aware of—was
Daniel. The strength of his features, the dark

curl of his hair, the absurd length of his eye-lashes and the growing heat in his eyes. A step closer to him and she was enmeshed by his aura, focused on the breadth of his chest, the toned masculinity of the sinews of his arms…

The sound of a man's throat being cleared, fol-lowed by the uttering of their names, broke the spell and she turned, pinning a smile in place.

'I am your guide for the tour. My name is Marco.'

'Pleased to meet you.'

'Follow me. As you know, this part of the pal-ace is a separate tour—I will be showing you the nitty-gritty, the less salubrious side, as well as the places where the real work was done over the centuries.'

As the guide moved forward Daniel looked down at her. 'You're sure about this?'

'Yes.' She'd done some research before they left, and although there was a definite risk that some of the rooms might trigger panic, she wanted to give it a try. 'I want to see the be-hind-the-scenes reality as well as all the trea-sures and art-work.'

Plus the tickets had been gifted to them, and

she had no wish to explain why she hadn't done the tour now they had got this far.

Kaitlin followed the guide through the narrow door and into the *'pozzi'*, and gave a shudder as she looked round in horror at the tiny stone-walled cells; their only ventilation small round holes. She saw the drawings on the wall—depictions of the prisoners' despair. Moisture sheened her neck and for a horrible moment the walls seemed to close in, the dank atmosphere blanketed her and terror rippled her body with memories.

The turn of a lock…the cloying feeling of powerlessness…the remembered pain as she'd repeatedly thumped the door until she'd realised no one would come. No one would rescue her.

She shook her head and focused on Marco's words, tried to remember that prisoners in times gone by had had it way worse than she had during her ten-day incarceration.

Then Daniel enclosed her hand in his and his deep voice offered reprieve.

'Would it be possible to move on, Marco? I suffer from a touch of claustrophobia and these walls are enough to cause me discomfort.'

'Of course, of course. Let us move on.'

For the next half an hour Kaitlin was transported back in time as they walked the chambers where the Council of Ten—a group of elected men with immense power—would have convened, rooms where they would have made life-and-death decisions, plotted and schemed. Then they toured the spacious Chamber of the Secret Chancellery, with its magnificent mirrored upper doors and cabinet-lined walls.

And the whole time the knowledge that Daniel still held her hand firmly in his grasp burned in her with a small white light of awareness. The sane Lady Kaitlin part of her told her that this was a public place and they were courting disaster. Yet his grasp made her feel safe, secure, protected, and therefore it behoved her to hang on. After all, there was no meaning to it—it was simply a tactic to keep panic at bay, the equivalent of a stress ball, nothing more.

You're kidding yourself, warned the voice of reason. Because if his grasp was warding off panic it was also ushering in other sensations: a warmth, a thrill, a delicious ripple of sensation reminiscent of their time walking through

Barcelona hand in hand. And look where *that* had ended up.

Yet as they explored the horror of the torture chamber, known as the Chamber of Torment, and listened to the chilling stories from the guide, she shifted closer to Daniel's bulk, remained there as they viewed the wood-panelled prison cell that had once housed Casanova himself, before his daring escape.

Only once the tour was over and they'd returned to the majesty of the main rooms of the palace did she drop his hand, forcing herself to do so without so much as tremor. Simply a cool smile.

'Thank you Daniel. Having something to hold did help.'

'Glad to be of service.'

It was a service she must not allow herself the luxury of using too often, or her stupid body would get the wrong idea. Distance—she *had* to keep her distance.

CHAPTER ELEVEN

FOR HOURS KAITLIN did manage to do exactly that—to maintain distance. As they toured the rest of the palace she submerged herself in the spectacular splendour of the Doge's apartments, in the ornate gold interior of the rooms, the impossible to describe detail of the frescoes, the sheer splendour of the art.

'Glad you came?' Daniel asked as they emerged onto the Bridge of Sighs.

'Yes. Truly. Thank you.'

'You're welcome.'

They paused on the bridge. 'Why is it called the Bridge of Sighs?' Kaitlin asked, testing herself as she looked into the chill green of the water. If she wanted to enjoy Venice she had to get her head round the fact it was a water-based city.

'Prisoners crossing the bridge knew it would be their last taste of freedom and open air, so they are said to have sighed as they crossed it. Other people say it is the sigh lovers make. Legend has it that if you take a gondola ride under the Bridge of Sighs as the sun sets with your significant other and you kiss then your love will be eternal.'

'Lucky I don't believe in love, then, because there is no way on this earth I'm getting in a gondola. Or even a *vaporetto*. My enjoyment of Venice is going to be on land!'

'But your plan *is* to enjoy Venice?'

Kaitlin pulled in a breath. 'If you still want my company?'

There was a pause, and for a moment she wondered if she had just made a complete idiot of herself.

'Though if you would rather spend time alone here because of your dad and everything I understand.'

'Shh.'

Lifting a hand, he brushed a finger softly against her lips, and she froze at the exquisite sensation that ran through her, then backed a step away, looking around to make sure no one had seen. But the throngs of tourists had no interest in them—were too busy gazing at the Palace.

'I do still want your company.'

'Then why the hesitation? I don't want your pity because of what I told you.'

'You don't have my pity.' His lips turned up in a rueful twist. 'My hesitation was due to a momentary worry that I might succumb to the temptation to kiss you. The problem is, I want more than that.'

'Oh.'

Please kiss me.

Get a grip.

There could be no kissing. Though right now Kaitlin wanted him to kiss her with a yearning so great she could taste it. But that wasn't possible—she and Daniel weren't a normal couple on holiday in Venice, like so many of the men and women around them, who could stop and kiss whenever they liked.

Come to that they weren't a couple of any description. She was Lady Kaitlin Derwent— a woman who wanted an alliance that would bring glory to the Derwent name, who wanted a family, children, marriage. Daniel was a man who wanted success and all its trappings—a man who could offer no more than a few days of pleasure to any woman.

For Lady Kaitlin Derwent that pleasure would come at way too high a price. The gossip, the scandal, her parents' fury… And more than that there was the risk of losing herself—the risk that her whole being would unravel. Daniel represented danger and disorder. Any involvement with him would be too scary. It sent a skitter of anxiety through her whole body.

'You can't kiss me.' Her voice was breathless, a squeak of pure panic.

The rueful look on his face intensified. 'Don't look so troubled, Kaitlin. I understand that. Forget I said anything and let's focus on enjoying Venice. Agreed?'

'Agreed.' Pushing her doubts away, Kaitlin nodded.

How hard could it be not to kiss someone for two days?

Daniel glanced out of the latticed semi-circular window at the late-morning sunshine that glinted off the canal and rooftops of St Mark's

Square before turning to where Kaitlin sat at the round marble-topped table, pen tucked behind her ear.

'What would you like to do today?' He gestured at their now closed laptops and neat pile of papers. 'Now that we know the ball is completely under control.'

They had spent the morning checking and double-checking that the arrangements were in place and watertight.

'The rest of today is ours to do with as we choose.'

Kaitlin rose from the table and headed to the window, oh, so careful not to so much as brush past him. 'There is a part of me that's tempted to stay right here in safety, but most of me feels cautiously optimistic that I can deal with outside. I would like to go to the Scuola Grande di San Rocco, if that's OK with you? It's a little off the beaten track, but I'd love to see so many of Tintoretto's works under one incredible roof. '

'Sounds like a plan. I'll get directions, and we can always use our phones to navigate.'

He sat down and pulled his computer towards him to source exact directions—sure that for

Kaitlin the idea of getting lost would hold little appeal and might indeed trigger panic.

'Thank you.'

As he glanced at her he felt a funny little tug pull at his chest. Dressed in a blue lace dress that combined simple elegance and comfort, Kaitlin looked...relaxed—more relaxed than he could have imagined. Her glorious hair hung in loose waves to her shoulders, her green eyes held a glint of emerald and her body held minimal tension.

He glanced at the map of Venice and made some quick calculations. 'OK. Route mastered. Let's go.'

As they exited the hotel from the back entrance, walked through the peaceful courtyard and through the wrought-iron gates that led out onto a bustling Venetian street, Daniel glanced down at her. Her body held more tension now, as they joined the crowds, and he couldn't help but wonder how hard it must be for her to contain her panic—the amount of energy and strain she expended in simple day-to-day life.

'I know what you need. You need pizza.'

'I do?'

'Yup. We'll get takeaway pizza and eat it whilst we watch the world go by.'

Twenty minutes later he had made good on his promise and they were seated in a small court-yard—a pocket-sized garden of tranquillity. The scents of oleander and laurel mingled with the pungent tomato sauce of the pizza, and the background sounds of the fountains merged with the noise of St Mark's square just metres away.

Kaitlin sat on a bench and took a bite of pizza. 'This is fabulous.' For a while they ate in companionable and appreciative silence. Until she wiped her mouth with a napkin and turned to face him. 'You keep asking how I am. Now it's my turn. How are *you*?'

'Fine.'

A shake of her head indicated disbelief. 'You told me that last time you came to Venice it made you feel melancholy. What about this time? I'm not trying to pry.' Her expression was soft, pensive. 'But you have helped me—you *are* helping me, so much—and I want you to know that if I can reciprocate I want to.' She sighed. 'Not in a tit-for-tat way—more in a…I'd like to.' A shake of her head. 'I can't believe how garbled I'm being.'

'It's OK. I get it.'

Ironically, he did—way more than he got her carefully thought out sentences, however clever or apposite they might be. *This* Kaitlin was real, genuine, and he didn't want to close the conversation down. Because to do so would be to send the real Kaitlin away.

'Last time I came here was eight years ago—I was much younger and more emotional and it felt like a pilgrimage. This time I'm older and wiser.'

This time he also had Kaitlin, but that was neither here nor there.

'I wish my parents had had this chance—a chance to make a go of it, enjoy the beauty of the city—but I can't change the past.'

'No. You can only face forward,' she said, quoting his words back at him. 'But the past is still important, because it shapes your future.'

'Your own choices shape your future.'

'Of course. But you can't deny the past has an effect. Even if you wish it didn't. You are a different person than the one you would have been if your father had lived.'

'So you don't believe our fate is ordained from birth?'

'Perhaps some of it is. Or maybe not "ordained" but made probable. It is more likely that I will mix in aristocratic circles because I am from an aristocratic family. But it's not set in stone. My sister Cora was never very interested in that side of things.' She tucked a stray strand of hair behind her ear. 'So it's not only our birth but also our family who influences us. After your father died I'm sure your grandparents must have had an impact on your life.'

'Unfortunately not.' The age-old anger flared in his gut. 'My mother had run away from her own family as a teenager—she would never speak of the reasons, but I assume her childhood was pretty horrific. My dad's family wanted nothing to do with us.'

'Why?'

'They thought my mother was beneath my father. When she got pregnant and they decided to get married my dad's parents were furious.

They asked him to choose between them and my mother.'

The irony of the situation caused bitterness to rise in his throat.

'He chose my mother, so they disowned him—fired him from his job in the family restaurant business and blackened his name. My dad took any job he could find, because he was determined to provide for us—for his baby, his family. He worked all hours because he was determined to succeed on his own. One of the jobs he took on was as a lorry driver—he was so exhausted he fell asleep at the wheel, the lorry crashed and he died. Luckily at least no one else was hurt.'

As he told the story he had almost forgotten he had an audience. His desire for the tale to have a different ending burned as deep as it had in childhood. Accompanied by the same sear of guilt.

A feeling of warmth permeated his senses, the scent of rose, the sense of comfort, as Kaitlin shifted closer to him on the bench, leant forward and touched his arm. 'Your poor, poor mum. The shock must have been awful—your dad sounds so vital, so strong. And poor you as well. To never have known him.'

'My mother told me about him. He was the love of her life—according to her, love at first sight *is* possible. She was a waitress in one of his family's restaurants—they met and *kaboom*.' The sound of his mother's voice echoed across the years. The click of her fingers as she'd said the word. 'They had so many hopes and dreams and plans—if it hadn't been for me their story would have played out differently.'

'It's not *your* fault.' Her voice was urgent; fervour brightened the green of her eye to emerald.

'It's not about fault. It is about fact. My grandparents cast him off because of the pregnancy. He was working all those jobs to provide for me.'

Kaitlin shook her head, studying his expression with way too much understanding, and discomfort caused him to shift on the wooden slats of the bench.

'It sounds to me as though your dad loved you, and it is a tragedy he didn't live to see the man you have become. But the fact is that it is *not* your fault.' As if sensing his unease, with her usual unerring social poise she changed tack.

'So, what were their plans and dreams? Did your mother tell you?'

'They wanted to set up a restaurant—here in Venice, where his family originated. Travel… have a brood of children.'

'So your dad was Italian?'

'Yes.'

'But you took your stepfather's surname?'

Easy does it.

This was why he should have never have embarked on this conversation. Perhaps the ambience of Venice, the flavour of might-have-beens, the sudden urge to keep his father's memory alive had all combined to loosen his tongue. The suspicion that in actual fact it was Kaitlin—her understanding, her sheer presence—that had caused the hitherto unheard of confidence-sharing unnerved him.

It was an unacceptable possibility—letting people close caused potential hurt to all concerned and it was time to bring this to a halt.

'I kept my mother's name.' In fact he had changed it when he'd left the States—had needed a clean start with no connection at all to his past. A past he had left behind.

Daniel screwed up his napkin with a savage scrunch and rose to his feet, saw Kaitlin's troubled look and pulled a smile to his face. This was not her fault—it was his. And he wouldn't let it happen again. From now on in this was about enjoyment of Venice—no more than that.

'If you're ready, I know the perfect place for dessert.'

As they walked back towards the hustle and bustle of St Mark's Square Kaitlin couldn't help but dwell on what Daniel had shared.

Next to her, she could sense the strength of his body and the vibration of frustrated anger, and she wondered about his current family situation. The way he had spoken of his mother suggested distance—she had no immediate sense of the woman whose life had been touched by such tragedy.

Walking closer to him, she wanted to soothe him, remembered how much comfort she had derived from human contact. So she slipped her hand into his. For a second his stride faltered, and then he returned the pressure and they kept walking until they arrived at a café.

Though 'café' seemed way too commonplace a word—this was a real, proper European coffee house.

'If I narrow my eyes to filter out the modern-day clothing I can imagine that we've stepped back in time.'

'This was once the haunt of the likes of Casanova, Proust and Charles Dickens. Lord Byron used to brood and breakfast here as well.'

'Where would you like to sit?'

Outside, tables and chairs were scattered under the colonnades, and an orchestra played classical music that further added to the sense of history.

'Wherever you prefer,' Daniel said.

'Let's go inside,' she decided. 'If the outside is so magnificent I can't imagine the inside.'

And indeed it did defy description. As they sat in the gilded interior, where vast mirrors, stuccos and paintings ranging from the Oriental to portraits vied for attention, listening to the strains of beautiful notes that wafted in from outside and mingled with the smells of cakes and pastries, Kaitlin felt joy touch her.

'This is incredible.'

She looked down at the sheer decadence of

her *gianduia* and pistachio *parfait* and dug her spoon into the concoction. Savoured the smallest bite, the cool, smooth texture, the tang of hazelnut complemented by the rich dark chocolate.

'I almost can't bear to actually eat it—it is so beautiful. And as for this hot chocolate…that is too mundane a translation. I think I prefer the Italian—*cioccolata calda con panna*.'

Daniel's face lit up in a grin and she felt the effect right down to her perfectly painted toes. 'Take as long as you like. You look like a little girl at her first birthday party.'

'That's how I feel.'

In fact she felt suddenly lightheaded, and she knew it was nothing to do with the sugar rush. It was to do with her sense of accomplishment and it was to do with Daniel. Danger tolled a bell in the deep recesses of her brain but Kaitlin ignored it, suddenly determined that nothing would spoil this day.

'That's awesome.' He lifted his espresso. 'Long may it last.'

For a moment she thought he might expound on his views on her getting help, but he didn't. Instead his gaze rested on her and something sparked in his eyes—something that warmed her from the inside out, made her want to hurl caution to the spring breeze. All that mattered was this moment in time, the glide of the tuxedoed waiters, their platters expertly balanced, the strum of the orchestra, the smell of cake and sugar mingled with the tang of rosemary, and the dark, bittersweet melting of chocolate on her tongue.

But most of all there was Daniel—his aura, his potency, his sheer being as his lips turned up into a smile that stole the breath from her lungs.

'You look happy.' The depth of his voice caressed her skin. 'And relaxed, and…' A chuckle accompanied the words. 'You have a smudge of sugar on the tip of your nose…'

Kaitlin reached into her bag for a pocket mirror and looked at her reflection. 'And a chocolate moustache,' she completed for him. 'I really *do* look as if I'm at a kid's birthday party.'

To her surprise a small laugh bubbled up, and then she couldn't quite help herself—scooping up a bit of whipped cream, she leant over and dabbed it on the end of Daniel's nose.

Surprise daubed his expression with a comical grimace as he wiped it off and her laughter bubbled over, erupting in a stream of giggles that she couldn't stem. A second later and he had joined in, with a deep belly laugh that caused the neighbouring customers to turn and look.

Then, as their laughter subsided, he grinned at her and Kaitlin could feel an answering smile tilt her lips as he reached out and gently swiped his finger down the bridge of her nose.

A tingle shot through her, and for a long moment their gazes intermingled before she hauled in breath. 'Thank you. I haven't laughed like that in a long time.'

'Neither have I.'

Those alarm bells clanged again.

Get it together.

This was *not* how Lady Kaitlin Derwent behaved.

'Right. Um…well, I guess I'd better get eating and we'd better get a move on. After all, we only have today.'

Regret twinged and she gave her head a small shake. They might only have today, but perhaps that meant she should enjoy every second, silence the alarm bells and live in the moment.

After all there could be no danger in wandering the streets of Venice chaperoned by throngs of fellow tourists.

Scooping up another exquisite bite, she smiled at him. 'Onward.'

CHAPTER TWELVE

ONWARD. DANIEL GLANCED down at Kaitlin as they left the café and for a scant second wondered exactly where 'onward' was taking them. Disquiet prickled his skin as he quenched the urge to clasp her hand in his again.

Ridiculous.

Kaitlin did not need to hold his hand—it seemed clear that her panic had at least temporarily been held at bay, granting her a reprieve.

So it was best that he held his distance and continued to ignore the attraction that hazed the air between them. Instead he focused on their environment—the washing hanging to dry from windows, the aromas of cooking, a woman in her doorway shelling peas, the scent of the canal and the snatches of conversation as they wandered the narrow streets lined with brightly painted houses.

But at increasingly regular intervals his attention strayed back to Kaitlin, to the vibrant splash of her hair, the grace with which she walked, effortlessly cool and elegant in the lace dress. A vibe radiated from her of relaxed, confident enthusiasm, and her green eyes sparkled as she looked around, absorbing the sights and sounds of the city, and an unwanted warmth spread through his veins and brought a scowl to his face.

'Is something wrong?'

Daniel glanced down and forced his expression to neutral as he saw the question in her eyes. 'Not at all. For a moment there I thought I'd got us lost, but I haven't. If I'm right we should arrive in the next few minutes.'

Her forehead creased into a small frown, as if she didn't believe his answer, but then she gave a small lift of her shoulders, indicative of a decision to leave well enough alone.

A few more twists and turns and… *'Voilà.'*

The stone and marble building of the Scuola Grande di San Rocco was a truly impressive example of Renaissance architecture—a fitting home for its incredible interior.

Kaitlin's green eyes widened, her movements

slow and deliberate as she stood in front of each painting. 'It's almost as if I am being pulled in by the depth of emotion, the fervour. It makes me feel...*humbled*.'

'This one defines the meaning of awesome,' Daniel said. 'In that it fills me with awe and incredulity at its sheer...vastness.'

Tintoretto's attention to detail combined with the overall message each image portrayed showed him to be master of artistry and allegory.

'It stuns me that one man could create all of this in one lifetime. The detail, the anguish, the dedication...' Her voice was soft with reverence. 'But also the intelligence and the thought he must have put into it—the way each individual picture is part of the overall panorama.'

She turned away from the paintings and looked up at him, her face alight with curiosity.

'Is that how you feel about your company? That it's like a work of art, or a sculpture that you've built up piece by piece?'

It was an interesting concept. 'I've never thought of it like that.' The burn of ambition had motivated him to focus on growth and money, but in a way Harrington Legal Services *was* a work of art—a tapestry of success. 'But, yes, HLS is my creation.'

And he was proud of it for reasons other than its success—he was proud of what it represented, of the fact all his employees shared its ethos and principles.

'One that you were driven to create. Just like a lot of artists paint because they have no choice.'

'I have a choice.' *Didn't he?*

'Do you? Your life is all about work. You don't holiday, you don't want a family...'

Her words were matter-of-fact, yet he fought an absurd urge to fold his arms in defensiveness.

'I'm not a holiday type of person. I get edgy. Bored.'

The thought flitted in his brain that he hadn't been bored in Scotland or here in Venice. Obviously because this was a *working* holiday, even if the work wasn't associated with the law.

'I prefer to work—it's a choice. As for family—that is also my choice. It's not for me.'

Kaitlin shook her head. 'How often do you drive your sports car? Or cars?'

'Often enough.'

But quite possibly not often enough to warrant

their price tag. In truth his cars were simply tokens that marked his climb up the ladder of success—an indication that he was as successful as his step-family, proof that he had enough lucre to support his mother and his half-sister in the lifestyle they had become accustomed to.

'I don't think you do. You told me that my panic imposes limitations on my life—maybe your drive to succeed imposes limitations on *yours*.'

As she walked over to placard headed 'The Life of Tintoretto' she gestured for him to follow.

'Look. Tintoretto had it all. He lived a long, prosperous life, married and had eight children, and even trained three of them to follow in his footsteps. Yet he managed to paint all this and way more. He had *balance*. I—'

Her words came to an abrupt cessation, her animation replaced by a frozen mask of terror, her body preternaturally still. He turned to follow her line of glazed vision, saw that a group of English tourists had entered—a man and two women, the man dark-haired and bearded with his sunglasses still on. His voice was loud and argumentative, and clearly he had been dragged here by his companions against his will. But he was paying no heed to Kaitlin, and he couldn't see what there was to trigger her panic.

No matter—Kaitlin swayed slightly and he could almost see her fight-or-flight instinct come to the fore.

'We're out of here,' he said, keeping his voice calm and even as he approached her. 'Come on, Kaitlin, start walking.'

She flinched away from him, backed up a step.

'I'll get you out of here. No problem. I'll keep you safe. No need to panic.'

The words came automatically and he was careful to keep his hands by his sides, sensing she had to come of her own choice. In the meantime he stepped in front of her, blocked her view of the man and hoped the group wouldn't approach.

'Let's walk. Easy does it.'

Kaitlin hesitated and he saw her eyes refocus, gaze up at the ceiling and then around her, before ending up riveted to his face. She puffed out a small sigh and started to walk.

The pace she set was a half-march, her usual poise ragged, hands clenching and unclenching as they stepped out into the early dusk. Casting a glance over her shoulder, another into the shadows, she increased speed.

After five minutes Daniel decided they had put enough distance between themselves and whatever or whoever had spooked her with such radical effect.

'Kaitlin—stop. Or at least tell me where you want to go.'

'Home.' A half-laugh. 'The hotel, I suppose. I need to be somewhere safe.'

'You *are*.' Without thought he turned and halted in front of her, and took her hands in his. 'Whilst you are with me you are safe. I will not let any harm come to you.'

A tug of her hands as she shook her head. 'Those are *words*, Daniel. Anyone can use words to manipulate, to lie...'

'Or to tell the truth. And that is what I am doing. You are safe. Right here, right now. If you want to go back to the hotel then that's where we will go, but we don't need to run there. If you want to stay out we can, and you will be safe. Trust me.'

Her breathing slowed as she met his gaze and he could almost see the cogs and wheels whirring in her brain.

Trust him. Kaitlin tried to think past the glut of emotions that clogged her brain. Logic told her to return pronto to the hotel, shut herself in her room and calm down. A deeper instinct wanted to stay with Daniel—to recapture the confidence and the freedom of earlier, to have a night in Venice. Shades of the past, of Barcelona…

No. This was different—she wasn't faking her identity and Daniel was no longer a stranger.

Her heart-rate thudded back to as near to normal as possible when he was this close and she made her decision. Maybe she'd regret it—most likely she would—but… 'I'd like to stay out.'

A squeeze of her hands and then he released one and retained the other in a clasp of reassurance. 'How does a night at a jazz club sound?'

'Perfect.' Once again warmth touched her at the way he seemed able to read her needs—a jazz club was far less likely to trigger panic than a standing-room-only bar packed with people, and the music would help.

For the journey there she simply followed Daniel, didn't so much as give any protest a thought when he clasped her hand in his because it felt *right*. The fear triggered in the *scuola* had abated, but her nerves were still frayed and memories danced in grotesque shadows at the back of her mind.

But the memories were held at bay by Daniel's presence, by both the reassurance and the thrill his touch bestowed.

The club itself was everything she could have wished for—both quirky and eclectic enough to push the past further away. Vibrantly painted walls were offset by dim illumination, the club's love of jazz clear in its themed memorabilia, a homage to artists past and present.

The proprietor showed them to a candlelit bistro-type table, secluded by the width of a Gothic column, and the tension drained from her body as she watched the band tune up, ate a selection of cold meat and cheese and bread, and listened to the notes jump and dance on the air, rebounding into her brain with a cleansing beat.

Then Daniel leant forward. 'Better?' he asked.

'Yes.'

'So what happened back there? Did you know that man?'

Reluctance to answer pressed her lips together, and then common sense prevailed. Daniel had made her a promise to keep her safe—he couldn't do that without facts.

'No. He reminded me of someone from my past and I went into panic freefall.'

With an effort she kept her tone light, tucked a tendril of hair behind her ear, focused on the tang of wine on her tongue.

'You can talk about it if you want. Maybe I'm a good choice, because after tomorrow our paths won't cross again.'

The words caused her an unexpected wince of hurt, a fluttery sensation in her chest, and for a second she would swear there was sadness in the twist of his lips.

Daft.

Daniel Harrington was no good for her—time spent with him seemed to have somehow frayed her entire Lady Kaitlin persona around the edges. Worse, she wasn't sure she cared. Because he was a good man—good enough that she was sorely tempted to take him at his word. To tell him about the incident that had changed her whole life's path, intrinsically altered her from the inside out.

But to do that she would have to take trust a whole skyscraper further.

He picked his drink up and lifted his broad shoulders. 'I understand if you can't trust me enough. That is a decision only you can make.'

As she picked up an olive and took a small bite she remembered what he had told her of his family—information she knew was personal to him. She remembered that he hadn't gone public with Barcelona, remembered how he had helped her these past days, allowed her a chance to experience Venice in a way that would have been impossible otherwise. She recalled how he had been in Scotland, with the teenagers. If she couldn't trust this man, who had such a sense of integrity, then all her remaining belief in human nature would shatter.

'I do trust you enough,' she said quietly. 'And I appreciate your offer to listen—maybe it *will* help.'

She swirled her drink round the glass, gazed down into it, unable to face him, to see his expression when she told him.

'Hey. Look at me. Whatever you tell me I will respect your confidence. And I won't judge you and I won't pity you.' Leaning over the table, he placed a gentle finger under her chin. 'I promise.'

Drawing in a shaky breath, she closed her eyes. Then opened them and forced herself to look into the deep blue depths of his.

'When I was thirteen I was kidnapped. I wanted to go to a concert and my parents said no. One of the staff, Natalie, offered to help me—I trusted her, and she helped sneak me out of the manor. Turned out it was all a plan to kidnap me.'

Daniel sat very still, but she could sense the anger that emanated from him, saw his hands clench into purposeful fists. 'You must have been terrified.'

'It took me a while to truly comprehend what

was happening. To this day I don't know where they held me—but I was there for ten days whilst they negotiated with my parents. The longer it went on, the more frustrated they got and the worse it was for me. Especially after I tried and nearly managed to escape.'

Kaitlin couldn't contain the shudder.

'Did they hurt you?'

Now there was no mistaking his anger, and that fury made her feel protected in a way she never had before. Her parents' anger had been directed at *her*, not at the kidnappers. The blame had been handed to her and she'd borne it for the past fourteen years.

'They threatened me. Natalie told them about my fear of water and they exploited that. Held me under in the bath. They also—'

Her voice broke as memories crowded in. The taste of sheer humiliation, the clammy sheen of bone-deep terror at the realisation of her powerlessness and her kidnappers' strength.

'They made me pose for photographs—threatened my parents that they would release them.'

'Oh, hell, Kaitlin. If I could get my hands on them I swear to you I'd make them pay.'

He rose and moved round the secluded table, sat next to her so he shielded her from anyone's view.

'I'm OK. It happened in the past. I was shaken today because that bearded man reminded me of one of the men who held me. Mostly I face forward.'

'You can't face forward if the demons are constantly at your back. First you have to deal with them.'

As she saw the determination on his face she wondered if he had dealt with whatever demons lay behind him. 'I have dealt with them. For the most part.'

'By yourself. I still don't understand why your parents didn't get you some help?'

'They couldn't risk the publicity—they were terrified of what the kidnappers would do with those photographs, and they were furious with me. If I hadn't sneaked out to go to that concert the whole situation wouldn't have arisen. It cost them a lot of money to get me back.'

Hearing the bitterness in her own words, she shook her head.

'No. That makes them sound terrible. Of course

they were glad to have me back in one piece. But as far as they were concerned I'd messed up, there had been terrible consequences, but they had sorted it out and we all needed to put it behind us and move on.'

'But they must have realised the experience had traumatised you—would traumatise *anyone*.'

'No, they didn't. They didn't want to talk about it, forbade me to tell anyone, ever, and that was that. So I figured out how to deal with it myself. As I got older I did some research into panic attacks and I have worked out various strategies for how to deal with it.'

Strategies that had worked just fine until Daniel had entered her orbit.

'So here I am.'

'Here you are and here's to you, Kaitlin.' He held up his glass. 'To your strength and determination.'

Shyness mingled with appreciation of his words and brought heat to her cheeks. 'Thank you. And thank you for listening.'

Sharing the experience that had clouded her

life for so long had drained her, and yet it had also brought her a strange feeling of peace.

'Now, I'm ready to go back to the hotel—if that's OK with you?'

'Of course it is.'

CHAPTER THIRTEEN

THEY WALKED BACK to the hotel in a silence that held comfort and an inevitable closeness. Daniel walked close to her, felt a surge of protectiveness towards this woman who was so much more than he could have imagined. The idea of what she had gone through fuelled anger inside him—at the staff member who had betrayed a young girl's trust, at the kidnappers themselves, and at the Duke and Duchess for their reactions. For allowing their daughter to take the blame for an atrocity perpetrated by others, for not giving her any help or sympathy or understanding.

'It's all right.' Kaitlin looked up at him, her face illuminated in the moonlight. 'I'm OK. I didn't tell you what I told you because I want you to be angry on my behalf. It's done.'

'Hey… You aren't meant to be comforting *me*!'

'I'm not. If I'm honest, I like it that you're angry on my behalf, because no one else ever has been. But I don't want your blood pressure to skyrocket whilst you brood on it.'

'It just makes me mad that they got away with it—that they are out there somewhere.'

'I have to believe that what goes around comes around—that karma will take care of them.' She moved a little closer to him. 'But now I think we should be enjoying Venice by moonlight.'

As they walked the magic of Venice seemed to swirl around them—the majesty of the darkened streets swathed in moonlight, the occasional sound of oars on the canal breaking the stillness alongside the laughter of a late-night reveller. And subtly the atmosphere changed. Daniel's anger faded away and the balm of the evening breeze, the rose scent she emanated, seemed to cast a spell he knew he should try and dispel.

But he couldn't. As they approached St Mark's Square—now nigh on deserted, vast and truly breathtaking in its illuminated splendour—it wasn't possible not to turn and pull her into his arms.

And as if Kaitlin felt exactly the same way—as if she too had been imbued by the same magical allure—she stood on tiptoe, her green eyes wide with wonder as she touched her lips to his.

That was all he had meant it to be—a brush of the lips—but her closeness, the warmth of her body, the taste of her lips, spun him into a vortex of desire and he deepened the kiss.

Kaitlin gave a small moan as her lips parted and he was lost. He tightened his arms around her, gathered her body flush against his. Need jolted his body as she twined her arms around his neck and whispered his name. Time lost all meaning as passion captivated them in an embrace that rocked his body and consumed his mind.

Until finally some small fragment of sense pervaded the enchantment, reminded him of who she was and gently he pulled away.

They stared at each other for a long moment, their ragged breaths mingling in the air.

Eventually she looked around and let out a sigh. 'We must have been mad, but right now I don't care.'

Her lips turned up in a smile so beautiful his breath caught.

'So what now?'

'That's up to you.' However much he wanted her, the decision had to be hers.

Her step was sure as she moved towards him. 'We have one more night—I want to make the most of it. Of this.'

'Are you sure?'

'I'm sure. It's a risk worth taking. If the reporters find out, so be it. I want this night. With you. If that's what you want too.'

'It is exactly what I want.'

A small, breathless laugh dropped from her lips. 'Then let's go.'

The short walk back to their hotel was achieved at a half-run, his urge to hold her hand restrained only by the knowledge that there was a chance that reporters and guests for the ball the following night might already have arrived.

As they approached Kaitlin slowed, and he could almost see her morph into the persona of Lady Kaitlin Derwent. He wondered whether that had been another defence mechanism against the after-effects of the kidnap.

They entered the hotel, where Roberto awaited them, discussed the ball and their plans for the following day without even a hint of impatience,

and then finally made their way across the lobby
to an elevator that began an excruciatingly slow
ascent.

Finally—*finally*—they reached the suite, entered and closed the door behind them.

'Now, where were we…?' he asked.

Stepping forward into his arms, she gave a
slow smile. 'I think we left off about *here*. But
we can make it even better if we move to the
bedroom.'

'Your wish is my command.'

With that he scooped her into his arms and
headed for the bed.

Kaitlin opened her eyes and for a second a tendril of panic coiled in her tummy. Then she remembered exactly where she was. The weight of
Daniel's arm cocooned her and she shifted gently on the sumptuous smooth silk of the sheet.
In repose he looked younger, one lock of dark
hair curled on his forehead, the craggy strength
of his features slightly softened by sleep.

She waited for regret to consume her but realised that in truth she repented nothing; she
couldn't feel *any* remorse over the beauty of the

past few hours. The passion and the laughter and the sheer pleasure—it had been a night that she would treasure the memories of for ever.

As for sharing her past with him… There was no regret over that either—no shadow of doubt that she could trust him to keep her confidence. She trusted him.

The realisation was shocking in its simplicity, terrifying in its complexity. Because she had broken a cardinal Lady Kaitlin rule.

Unfamiliar emotion crept up her veins, coursed through her body with unidentifiable sensations as she gazed at Daniel. Joy mingled with a yearning to lie down again in the safety of his arms, to wake him up and make love. To make him breakfast, to spend the day walking the streets of Venice hand in hand…

A new type of panic sparked and morphed into dread and disbelief.

What was she *doing*? Weaving a fantasy out of an illusion? The reality was that the night was over and so was her time with Daniel. It was time to assume Lady Kaitlin Derwent's mantle and get back to her routine—the life she had so carefully and painstakingly built up. She could not, *would* not let that crumble, and she would not, *could* not fall in love with Daniel Harrington.

Daniel opened his eyes and met her gaze sleepily. 'Morning.'

'Good morning.'

Surprise banished sleep and a small frown creased his forehead. 'What's wrong?'

'Nothing is wrong.'

Everything was wrong, and her brain threatened to short-circuit as emotions overloaded it. The primary emotion was horror at her body's treachery. She had never meant to fall in love— this was meant to have been an interlude, time outside time, the opportunity to experience physical attraction. Not this crazy freefall. She had to get out of here before it took hold. Before she did something super-crazy.

Before he figured it out.

From somewhere she summoned reserves of pride—the idea of discovery was a humiliation impossible to contemplate. So she had to dig deep and locate Lady Kaitlin—who disdained love as a messy, unpleasant, unnecessary component to life and relationships.

Play the part. Image is everything.

Holding the sheet to her, she leant over in a desperate bid to find at least her bra and knickers.

'I've woken up with my head buzzing with all the things we need to get done for the ball. Plus I need to get back to my room and make sure it looks like I slept there.'

Finally her fingers found her bra, and somehow she wriggled into it whilst shielding herself as best she could with the sheet.

'Kaitlin.'

Don't look at him.

If she could just make it to the sanctuary of her room she would be able to get herself together.

He swung himself out of bed and she resisted the temptation to close her eyes, to block out the masculinity, the clean muscular lines of his body. A body that had given her so much joy.

'Let me help.' He picked the rest of her clothes up from the floor and placed them on the bed.

Scooping up the clothes and tucking the sheet around her, Kaitlin sought refuge in the sumptuous bathroom. She avoided her reflection in the ornate gilded mirror as she scrambled into her dress. It would all be fine once she'd had a chance to shower and put on fresh clothes and focus.

On her return to the bedroom she found Daniel standing by the door, clad now in jeans, leaning back on the wall.

'What's the rush? This doesn't have to be awkward.'

'It's not awkward. It's realistic. We have to make sure no one suspects what happened last night.'

Not that she cared—all that mattered now was the imperative to curtail the rot of unwanted emotion. Filter her heart of even the tiniest propensity towards love. To do that she needed to be Lady Kaitlin Derwent with all the fibre of her body and soul.

Confusion flickered in his blue eyes and then it was gone. He pushed himself away from the wall and nodded. 'Of course. I suggest we go downstairs in half an hour—I'll see if Roberto can chaperone us over breakfast.'

'Perfect.'

The irony was not lost on her—*perfection* did not encompass the prickle of incipient tears or add weight to her heart. More stupid pointless feelings that she had to stop, crush, destroy. No matter what it cost her she would find her even keel once more—all she had to do was get through the next hours and it would be over. Daniel would be banished from her life and her mind.

There was no alternative.

Yet as she surveyed her reflection that evening, prior to the meet-and-greet, tears still threatened to seep.

Why had she chosen lace for her ball gown? The floor-length, deep V-necked dress was beautiful, it was true—French lace with a floral motif over a nude silk lining. The top half hugged her figure, a slim black band emphasised her slender waist and the skirt flared to the floor. The back view was equally demure, with a bit of sass provided by the keyhole opening.

But the lace reminded her too much of the night before—the short blue dress, sun-kissed by Venice, being slipped off her shoulders in an urgent sweep of Daniel's strong hands, the sensation against her skin as it fell to the floor…

Stop.

Different dress. Different night. Different woman.

Tonight Lady Kaitlin Derwent would prevail.

The night took on an *Alice in Wonderland* quality, and she really wouldn't have been surprised to see a white rabbit materialise amongst the bejewelled, designer-clad guests. The ballroom seethed with glamour, amid the pop of champagne corks and under the brilliant glitter of the glorious neo-baroque chandeliers.

Through it all Kaitlin conversed and smiled, made witty and scintillating conversation, and felt the balm of being Lady Kaitlin heal her. From somewhere she found the dignity not to let her gaze follow Daniel's powerful form as he too played his part—the host with the most.

Yet some inner radar gave her an unerring insight into his exact location at any point...some hyper-awareness of him.

'Good-looking devil, isn't he?'

Kaitlin found the correct smile for the three-times Oscar-nominated actor, gorgeous in a dress that shimmered silver. 'There are a number of men here who could be described as such.'

'Daniel Harrington... He doesn't usually grace

events like this—in fact he's a bit of a dark horse. Is he yours, darling, or can I see if I can win his favour?'

The demon of jealousy tore its claws across her heart, but Lady Kaitlin didn't waver. A slight rise of the eyebrows, exactly the right touch of aristocratic hauteur offset by a smile that indicated understanding. 'He's as free as the proverbial bird, as far as I'm aware.'

Surely that must be the worst of this evening? But no... Next up was the auction where she stood next to Daniel, her cheeks aching under the weight of her smile, her vocal cords straining to deliver. But she did it. She managed to get over the impact of him, the smell of him, the memory of him.

Because as they bantered and delivered just the right sales pitch she remembered the teens she had met and bonded with, and all those other children out there who would benefit from this auction, and she threw herself into it heart and soul.

All she wanted at the end was to be allowed to leave and seek the sanctuary of her room, but that wasn't possible.

'And now let the dancing begin! And I'd like to invite our gracious hosts to open the proceedings with the waltz which I understand from Daniel you danced so beautifully at your brother's wedding, Lady Kaitlin.'

Please, no. This had to be some sort of joke. But, no—Roberto beamed at her and Kaitlin realised that the nightmare scenario had, against all the odds, got worse.

Daniel turned to her. 'I would, of course, be honoured.'

He held out his hand and his blue eyes glinted with challenge and more than a hint of anger. It enabled her to move towards him, hand outstretched.

'Likewise.'

As they walked to the dance floor she couldn't help but ask.

'Was this your idea?'

'No. Roberto asked me if I could waltz. If I'd known what he proposed I wouldn't have said yes. The only reason I can dance is that my PA dragged me along to classes when her husband somewhat conveniently broke his leg just before they were about to embark on a course. I won't disgrace you—don't worry.'

In truth Kaitlin was more worried about disgracing herself as the strains of Strauss's waltz began and they took to the floor. Poignancy pierced her as she placed her hand in his, the gap between their bodies so small and yet so full of significance. Because it was a gap that they would never close again.

For an instant she wasn't sure she could do it; she wanted to drop his hand and run but that wasn't possible. Dammit, she had too much pride. She could picture the headlines, taste the humiliation. Reporters would no doubt attribute it to her feelings for Prince Frederick, but Daniel wouldn't. He would guess the truth and she wouldn't let that happen. All this emotion had to be stopped, controlled, bottled up—starting now.

But as she stepped forward in one graceful, fluid movement she could swear she heard the crack of her heart.

Finally the night was over. The music, the chatter, the thud of the auctioneer's gavel and the sound of shoes on the dance floor were just faint memories that lingered like wraiths.

Daniel looked across at Kaitlin, standing in the shadows of the balcony that overlooked the ballroom, leaning against the ornate railings with the backdrop of silk hangings behind her.

'There's nothing left to do,' he said.

No one else remained. The last tasks had been completed, the last guest had departed, the staff had gone to recapture their strength for breakfast in a few scant hours. The silence was almost eerie, broken only by the thud of his heart as he surveyed her—so very beautiful in the lace concoction that showcased her poise and emphasised the vividness of her hair.

Confusion churned in his gut as he tried to work out what the hell had happened that morning to make Kaitlin so unapproachable, to make her withdraw and remain behind that mask of aristocracy.

'We need to talk.'

She turned in one graceful movement, her expression unreadable. 'No we don't. The ball is over and now we'll go our separate ways.'

Separate ways. The words filled him with a sudden bleakness.

'Then before we do that I'd like to talk.'

'There is nothing to talk about.'

'I disagree.'

She hesitated and then shrugged—a fatalistic lift of her shoulders. 'OK. Talk.'

'I want to know what happened this morning.'

A roll of her green eyes. 'Nothing happened except the fact that the night was over. It's time to face forward and that means saying goodbye. It's time for us both to get back to real life. *Normal* life.'

Something was wrong; his senses were on edge. And it wasn't only something wrong with Kaitlin—frustration built inside him at the idea of the vibrant woman he had come to know these past days morphing back into Lady Kaitlin Derwent.

'Is that really what you want—to go back to your "normal" life?'

'Yes, it is.'

'Then it shouldn't be.'

The frustration, the knowledge that he didn't want to say goodbye, the fact that he felt befuddled by emotions he didn't understand all made his voice sound harsh. But he didn't care.

'You are more than that, Kaitlin—you have the potential to soar. This past week you've been out of your comfort zone and in your element. You can be whatever you want to be.'

'I already am who I want to be.'

'Rubbish. I don't believe that you want to go back to that art gallery and wait until your parents identify your next eligible husband.'

Her wince was as palpable as her anger, and he almost regretted the starkness of his words. Almost, but not quite. Because the idea of Kaitlin entering that gilded cage made anger roil in his gut and caused his fists to clench.

An answering fury flashed back at him as her hands slammed on the curve of her hips. 'And what is so wrong with that, if it gives me what I want? A family. Children to love and cherish.'

Suddenly all his anger drained away, replaced by a sudden wish that *he* could give her what she wanted alongside the bleak knowledge that he couldn't. For one fleeting moment he tried to imagine it—but even the thought sent a cartwheel of panic through him. He was a man who had brought sorrow to the family he had—family was not for him. It was too messy, too complicated...too demanding.

But perhaps there was *something* he could do for Kaitlin. 'It doesn't always work out like that.'

'What do you mean?'

'My mother entered a gilded cage, made a deal—an alliance with my stepfather. After my father died she had no one to turn to and a baby on the way. She kept working as a waitress until the last possible moment but it wasn't easy. And it didn't become easier after I was born. She met my stepfather—he was older than her, he was rich and he was powerful and he wanted her. So she made a deal with him and married him. She did it for me—so that I could have everything in life.'

Guilt twisted its ever-present dagger once more—a reminder that love led to pain.

Kaitlin stepped towards him, the light of the ornate chandelier glinted off her Titian hair, bathed her skin in a golden glow, as she placed a hand on his arm. 'Maybe she did it for herself as well. I can't imagine how desperate and lonely she must have felt.'

'She didn't do it for herself. My stepfather is in the mob.'

Kaitlin's mouth formed a circle of surprise. 'The *mafia*?'

'Yes.' The fact brought an extra burn of shame. 'A bona fide criminal and my mother knew it. He wanted more children and she wanted a big family and he promised that he would give me the benefits of wealth—a luxurious lifestyle and an excellent education with all the extras.'

Impossible to blame his mother for her acceptance when it had been done for love of *him*.

'But every penny of his money came from the proceeds of crime. My mother isn't a bad person—she did it for me because she could see the way her life was headed and she couldn't see a better way out.'

'But…what happened? You aren't still connected to the mob, are you?'

'No. I walked away when I was eighteen—when I realised the deal was that I would go to law school and then work for the family, to protect the criminals. Until then I had turned a blind eye, but I couldn't play an active part.'

His skin prickled in recognition of the hypocrisy of his own culpability. He'd reaped the benefits of his stepfather's crimes and then refused to help him in return.

'I told my stepfather I would pay him back but that I wanted to go legit—make my own way. He went ballistic.'

It was then that he'd seen the man his stepfather could be—the side of him he kept away from his family, the part of him that had allowed him to rise in the ranks of the mafia. Even now he could feel the ripple of fear and shock as he'd faced the man he had believed cared for him.

'I'm not sure what would have happened if my stepbrother hadn't stepped in.'

'What did you do?'

'They told me I had a choice. I either had to comply or they would turn their backs on me. By which they meant I would no longer be part of the family—I would be as good as dead to them. I left.'

'But your mother…'

'I haven't seen my mother or my half-siblings since. I send a birthday card every year, and this year I asked her to come to Barcelona. It's ten years ago, and now I have the means to support her and my siblings, to match my stepfather's wealth. But she didn't come. Instead one of the family goons came—with a message. No one wants to meet a ghost. I am still dead to them and that is the way it will remain.' He shrugged. 'They're right. I made my choice to walk away. I was a fool to expect her to come running when I asked her after what I did.'

'No. You weren't a fool. I cannot imagine the pain it caused you to walk away. And you were right to try for a reunion—everything you told me about your mother makes me *know* that she must still love you. Life isn't black and white—it is not as simple as you walking away so she can never forgive you. But maybe first you need to forgive *yourself.*'

The near anguish in her voice as she tightened her clasp on his arm, moved closer, recalled him to the here and now. He saw the compassion in her eyes and for a heartbeat he wanted to step forward and hold her, let her hold him, accept her warmth and offer her...

Offer her what?

Ironically enough, he had nothing to offer her—just as he had nothing to offer his mother.

What Kaitlin deserved was love—the type of love that had existed between his parents. All he could give her was the benefit of experience and hope that he could prevent her from making the same errors his mother had made.

Stepping back, he pulled away from her clasp, forced his expression into neutral. 'I didn't tell you any of this for sympathy or analysis.'

Hurt flickered across her eyes but he forced his arms to remain by his side.

'I told you because I want you to understand that the type of alliance you are thinking about can backfire. My mother gained security and a family, but at a price—she's had a loveless marriage, endured humiliation as part of the fabric of her very being and lived off the proceeds of crime. She did it for me, and I repaid her by walking away. It is that black and white. So sometimes choices, however good they sound on paper, turn out to have far-reaching consequences. You deserve better than an alliance, Kaitlin—you deserve love. You deserve what my parents had.'

Her fingers twined in the dramatic sweep of her gown and her mouth opened in preparation for speech. Then came that small characteristic shake of the head and she pressed her lips together in a gesture he had come to know and love—

His feet froze to the plush carpet and his limbs grew heavy with shock. *Love?* The word wasn't in his lexicon and he didn't want it to be. *Did* he? His hand rose almost of its own volition and he forced it down. Words hovered on his tongue in a tangle and he swallowed them. He didn't have time for love—didn't understand the concept or what went with it. Couldn't offer something he didn't have the ability to give.

She raised her eyes to his, brilliant with a glitter he didn't understand. 'What about you, Daniel? Don't *you* deserve love as well?'

'No.' The syllable reverberated in the confines of the balcony with a harsh echo. 'I don't want love—neither to give or receive it.'

'You see, neither do I. But I *do* want children. So, I truly appreciate everything you have said, and I won't enter into any alliance unless I have a watertight exit route that enables me to take my children with me.'

He felt frustration mixed with the bitter tang of failure as she backed away.

'I also appreciate the past days and I truly wish you a happy life—I hope you get to see your mother and your siblings again. Goodbye.'

Words tumbled about in his brain, emotions churned in his gut and he knew they needed to be dispelled, eradicated, because they could do neither Kaitlin nor himself any good. So he would exit from her life, go back to his own—to a life ruled by his sheer will to succeed, make his company even bigger and better, grow his own personal fortune, buy a car, a yacht—whatever it took to prove he'd made it.

'Goodbye, Kaitlin. I wish you happiness.'

For a heartbeat she stood stock-still and he etched her image into his brain, and then she turned and left the balcony, her back ramrod-straight, the click of her heels echoing and fading with finality.

CHAPTER FOURTEEN

KAITLIN TOLD HERSELF to be strong. She recalled the words of the counsellor she'd been seeing for the past three months—a woman who had helped her in ways she couldn't possibly have helped herself.

'Sometimes the safe option isn't the right one.'

Pushing her shoulders back, she entered the lounge where her parents sat. For an instant guilt touched her—the Duke and Duchess were getting older, and for all their faults their love and pride in the Derwent name and heritage was real.

'Kaitlin.' Her mother didn't bother with preliminaries. 'We have news for you. We believe there is a possibility that Prince Frederick may consider a renewal of his offer to you.'

The news was not a shock—in the past three months Prince Frederick hadn't been seen with any other eligible women, but then again neither had he contacted Kaitlin.

'So,' continued the Duchess. 'We will arrange a dinner, ask the Prince and his two brothers—and others, of course.'

'I'd be happy to attend a dinner but...' Kaitlin hauled in breath. 'But I am not interested in a renewal of Prince Frederick's offer.'

'Excuse me?'

For the first time in Kaitlin's memory the Duchess looked shocked, her mouth agape, her usual calm and serene beauty marred by the twist of her lips.

'I don't want to marry Prince Frederick or any other prince.' More to the point, she *couldn't*. Because it wouldn't be fair to anyone—least of all herself—not when she loved Daniel.

It was a love that had endured her most persistent attempts to remodel it, purge it, suppress it. Instead his image permeated her being, her dreams. The idea of an alliance with anyone else curdled her soul.

'You will do as we say, Kaitlin.'

'No, Mother. I won't. I am sorry to let you down but I cannot marry the Prince—though I am happy to see him and explain the situation to him.'

The Duchess pursed her lips, clearly for once without words.

'Now…' Kaitlin glanced at her watch. 'I need to go. I'm meeting Cora.'

It was time to share some things with her sister, lay some ghosts to rest before she embarked on the next phase of her plan.

Daniel stared down at the two items on his desk—each one a sucker-punch to the gut.

Item one—a newspaper article that featured a picture of Lady Kaitlin Derwent and Prince Frederick in close conversation under the caption: *'On Again?'*

The Duke and Duchess of Derwent entertained in lavish style and their guests included the Lycander brothers—including, of course, Lycander's ruler, Prince Frederick, who was seen in deep conversation with Lady Kaitlin, prompting speculation that the couple might seek to rekindle their romance.

Since the split Prince Frederick has kept a

*low profile, and not so much as one woman
has been seen on the former playboy's arm.*

Daniel stared down at the photo, scrutinised
Kaitlin's expression for the umpteenth time and
still derived nothing from it.

So on to item two—a note on delicate blue
paper that he could swear bore a touch of her rose
scent. Fanciful idiocy of a type that occurred with
depressing regularity—wherever he went there
seemed to be echoes of his time with Kaitlin.

He read the note. Again.

Dear Daniel
*Forgive the short notice, but I wonder if you
could meet me in Barcelona this Saturday?*
  *Given the lack of notice, if you can't make
it I will, of course, understand. I will be at
the hotel where we met at six p.m.*
Best wishes
Kaitlin

Best wishes—what the hell did *that* mean?
Why did she want to meet? To tell him of her
new alliance with the Prince? Why Barcelona?

The only way to find out was to go.

* * *

Lady Kaitlin Derwent, poster girl for the aristocracy, daughter of the Duke and Duchess of Fairfax, stared at her reflection and wondered if…no,
knew that she had run mad. There could be no
other explanation for the fact that she was standing here, in this glitzy Barcelona hotel room,
about to act in a way so wildly out of character
that she could barely believe her presence here.

Yet it felt so *right*—more than that, it felt in
character, like the real Kaitlin. But that didn't
prevent the rush of nerves, the pounding of her
heart as she looked at the wall-mounted clock
and saw that it was six o'clock. One last glance
at the simple jeans and T-shirt ensemble she'd
picked, after choosing and discarding countless
other outfits, and then she turned, exited the
room and headed down the stairs.

Entered the lobby and stopped.

There he was, and it took all her will-power
not to run across the marble floor and launch
herself into his arms. That wasn't how this was
going to play out—Daniel wasn't that sort of a
man.

'Daniel.'

'Kaitlin.'

For a timeless moment they stood and stared at each other, and a sense of imminent sadness touched her. Daniel looked wary, aloof, and not at all like a man who was happy to see her.

For a second she was tempted to abandon the plan, recalling all the reasons why it truly sucked, but then she gritted her teeth. If she didn't do this she would regret it for the rest of her life. Or so Cora had assured her, anyway.

'Shall we?' he asked as he gestured to the bar.

'Yes. Actually, no. Let's walk. So, how have you been?'

The banality of her question was almost unbearable, but she wanted some time to absorb his presence, to look at him, to revel in his nearness even if her feelings clearly weren't reciprocated.

'Fine. You? You look well.'

'I *am* well. That was part of what I wanted to tell you. I took your advice. I went and found myself a therapist—one recommended by the Cavershams, in fact. She has been fantastic—and apparently I'm not a lost cause.'

It had been balm for her soul to realise exactly

how far she had come by herself, and to see how much further she could now go.

'I'm pleased, Kaitlin. That took courage. But I never doubted you had that.'

'Thank you.'

'You said that's partly why you wanted to meet me. What was the other reason?'

Hurt touched her—clearly Daniel wanted to cut to the chase and close this down as soon as possible. Yet there was a tension in him, as if he were reining himself in, exerting every ounce of his iron will. There was a rigidity to his shoulders, a tension to his jaw that she couldn't read. Doubts jostled and hustled her brain.

'Could we stop somewhere?' Glancing round, she realised they had wandered to the Magic Fountain of Montjuïc—one of Barcelona's top attractions. 'We could watch the show whilst we talk.'

Perhaps the beauty of the spectacle would give her courage or bring her luck.

Daniel nodded and led the way to the steps opposite the fountain, where they seated themselves in the anonymity of the throng of tourists.

'Go ahead.'

For a moment she inhaled the spicy scents of the food being sold by the numerous vendors who hawked their wares. She watched the acrobatics of the street entertainers, sought and found the courage of her conviction that she needed to be honest with this man.

'I wanted to tell you that Frederick and I—'

'Don't do it.'

The urgency in his voice effectively rendered her speechless for a moment, until understanding dawned.

'I know you don't think I should make an alliance, enter a gilded cage, and I wish I had told you in Venice how much I appreciated you confiding your mother's situation to me.'

He made a dismissive noise, brushed his hand over his head and clenched his fists as he leant forward. 'That's not what I meant. I meant don't marry Frederick because I love you.'

The words stunned her, and for a long moment she was sure her ears must have deceived her. 'I...I... Excuse me?'

'I love you, Kaitlin—I know you don't want love, but there you have it. I *love* you. The past three months have been hell. I've missed you and nothing cures it—I've dreamt of you, thought about you. About the way you press your lips together, the way your face lights up when you smile, the glorious intensity of your eyes, the way you walk, your strength, your stubbornness, your...your *everything*. I love you.'

'But...*how*?'

'I don't know.'

His expression was so flummoxed that it startled a small laugh from her lips.

'I thought I was incapable of love, but then you came along and you changed everything. You slipped under my guard and under my skin right from that first night in Barcelona. I fought it all the way, but now I don't want to fight it any more. Loving you is a joy.'

'But what changed your mind? Why do you want to stop fighting it?'

The first scratching of joy was beginning to unfurl inside her, but caution prompted the fear that this was an illusion—that Daniel had mistaken love for some other emotion.

'Because I realised you were right. Life isn't black and white and love isn't a tangible thing that I can conquer or deal with the way I can deal with a court case. Which is why I went to see my mother.'

'Oh, Daniel. Tell me.'

As he spoke the scene played out before Kaitlin's eyes…

Daniel parked the hire car and climbed out, wondering why he hadn't done this before. Did he truly believe his family would shoot him on sight?

Seeing the house he'd grown up in brought back a surge of memories that replayed in his mind like a cinematic reel.

Taken alone, they were happy memories, yet all tainted now with the knowledge of hindsight.

Kaitlin's words echoed in his brain. 'Life isn't black and white.'

Yet for so long to him it had been… But now here he was—he had no idea if he would be allowed entry, but at least he would have tried.

More than aware that there would be people watching his every move, he moved away from the car and walked to the door.

Walk as though you have the right to be here.

He could only hope his stepbrother could see him now. Knocking on the door with the shiny brass knocker, he could feel the accelerated thud of his heart as he heard the approach of foot-steps.

The door swung open and shock glanced through him. Shock and relief and near disbelief.

'Danny...' His mother's soft voice, her laven-der scent, her beauty that had worn the scourges of time. 'Come in.'

'I wasn't sure if you would see me.'

'You asked for an hour of my time, a chance to say the goodbye we never had time to say before. What mother could refuse that? Let me look at you, Danny. You have grown into a fine man.'

'My stepfather doesn't think so.' The words of bitterness were out before he could stop them.

'Antonio knows you are here. He understands that I need to see you.'

'But just this once?'

'That is my will, Danny.'

'Why?'

'Because I look at you and see all you have achieved. We are your skeletons in the closet— the people who can bring you down. How would it look if your colleagues, your clients, discov-ered you were once part of the Russo family?'

278 CLAIMED BY THE WEALTHY MAGNATE

'That is my look-out, Mamma. If the choice now is between my family and my career I choose my family. I don't want to walk away again.'

'You don't understand.'

'Then explain to me.'

'When I married Antonio I made a deal, knowing what I knew about him. I will not renege on the deal I made when he has kept his part. Your stepfather is not a bad man, though he has done bad things. But things have changed since you left. Your brother, your sister—they will not enter the family business. This he agreed. Because he did not want to lose them like he lost you. Antonio was born into the business and he did not have the strength to break away like you did—part of his anger was because of that. I know my marriage was not based on love, but we have a bond, your stepfather and I, and I have loyalty. I am not choosing him over you, Danny. Try to understand that. And understand something else as well. I never once regretted the deal I made—I love you, and love is a joyful, wonderful emotion. Even when your father died I could never regret loving him, knowing him.

And without that love I wouldn't have you. Is there love in your life, Danny? All you have told me in your letters is about material success—incredible achievements—but I want there to be love in your life...'

Daniel looked across at Kaitlin. 'It was as if the scales had dropped from my eyes and instead of black and white I could see the world in shades of colour.'

He gestured to the fountains, where the show had begun. Thousands of jets of water shot skyward, illuminated in various transitory hues and shades of colour.

'And I realised that to have love in my life is a glorious thing. And I could see you—an image of you by my side—loving, talking, laughing.'

'Then why didn't you come and find me?'

'Because I didn't want to complicate your life. You were so sure of your path, so sure you didn't want love, and I was...scared. But then I saw the article about you and the Prince. If you hadn't asked me here I would have come to find you, because I couldn't let you go through with it without telling you that I love you. Give me a chance, Kaitlin, and I swear I'll win your love.'

Now laughter bubbled up inside her. 'Daniel, you…you *idiot*. Why do you think I asked you back to Barcelona? To tell you that I love you! That I am *not* going to marry Prince Frederick.'

'You *love* me?'

Surprise flitted across his face and then he smiled—a smile that curled her toes and frizzed her hair.

'I do. With all my heart. You showed me how to be myself, how to stop hiding behind a façade, a persona that wasn't real. I didn't want love because I didn't feel I could handle the rollercoaster of emotions. After the kidnap all I wanted to do was shut my feelings down—all of them: the good, the bad and the ugly. It's how I coped.'

'Oh, sweetheart. That is understandable.'

'Maybe, but until I met you I'd succeeded only in achieving lockdown. Then Barcelona happened, and the feelings started, and I panicked, suppressed them. And then you arrived at Gabe's wedding… Since then, however hard I've tried—and, believe me, I've tried—I haven't been able to stop them. It's like the hydra—I chop one down and two more sprout in their place. That's why I had to get away after Venice—to try and build Lady Kaitlin back up.'

'What happened?'

He pulled her closer and she revelled in the ability to put her head on his shoulder, to touch him, to hold him.

'It didn't work. The feelings refused to go away, refused to be squashed or shut down. I missed you so much it hurt. But I didn't know what to do. I was scared. So I decided I needed to sort myself out. Work out who I was in case I didn't love you, in case I'd just been dazzled by physical attraction. So I found a therapist, talked to the Cavershams about setting up more workshops, changed my gallery hours to part-time. But through it all I couldn't stop thinking about you. The more I achieved, the more I missed you. I wanted to tell you everything. Then, when my parents suggested a reunion with Prince Fredrick…'

His grip around her tightened and she shifted closer to him in reassurance.

'I knew that no matter what I would *never* go back to being the Kaitlin who wanted an alliance, and I knew I had to have the courage to tell you how I feel. I needed to tell you. I wanted you to know that whether you want to receive love or not you have it. I spoke to Cora as well—told her about the kidnapping.'

Her voice broke slightly—the scene with Cora had been heart-wrenchingly emotional but it had restored the twins' bond that had been lost so long ago.

'She told me that love is so precious it should be given where it can. So that was what I came here to give it to you. My love.'

But she had never expected to have it reciprocated.

'I have no idea what comes next.' For a moment a small doubt shadowed her joy. 'I mean, what will happen to you if we start a relationship? The press will be interested and your family connections might come out.'

'It doesn't matter.' His voice was strong. 'I have already set the truth in motion. I won't *not* see my mother just because she thinks that is the way to protect me and my business. I have done nothing wrong, So over the past weeks I have held various meetings, explained the truth to my employees, and soon I will issue a statement explaining the truth. Of course there will be repercussions, but I believe I'll ride the storm.'

Her heart swelled at his sheer courage, integrity and self-belief. 'I know you will, and I will be riding it right beside you. But I promise I won't crowd you—I don't want you to make any deals or any rash promises. I know how you feel about children and marriage, and I'm good with that. I just want us to move forward together.'

'That is what I want. But I would *like* to make some promises. I promise to cherish and love you, body and soul. And as for children—that has changed, Kaitlin. Until now I was too scared of the responsibility that comes with parenting—I felt as though I had blighted my parents' life and in some way I felt that disqualified me from parenthood. Or maybe I was just too selfish—maybe I didn't want to feel so much love for another human being. But now…the idea of creating a child with *you*, of bringing a family up together…it feels right.'

'But not yet.' Kaitlin smiled. 'You see, now I can see that that isn't the be all and end all. I was being selfish too—I wanted children because I *did* want to give and receive love, and I couldn't think of another way. Now I have you, and that is plenty. I want to set up a new business. I want to travel. I want to learn how to be *me*. And I want to do all that with you by my side.'

'Then let's face forward and go into our future together.'

As he kissed her the fountain danced in a beautiful tapestry of colour against the night sky. And Kaitlin couldn't think of a better future than one shared with this wonderful man.

EPILOGUE

Six months later

DANIEL TIGHTENED HIS arm round Kaitlin's shoulders and felt the now familiar but still so welcome heady thrill of being able to hold her— the wondrous sense of amazed joy that they had found each other.

'You sure about this?' he asked as they both looked out over Venice's Grand Canal and then down at the gondola, manned by a smiling gondolier in a blue-striped top.

'A hundred per cent.'

'Then let's do it.'

Her beautiful face was set with concentration, and a small frown creased her brow as she climbed into the craft. But she smiled as he joined her and took her hand in his.

The gondolier set off and then stood at the front, a discreet distance away, facing forward and focused on his task.

'I can't believe I can do this now!' Kaitlin said, her voice light with happiness.

'I can. You've worked hard and you deserve this.'

Her panic attacks hardly ever surfaced now, and his pride and admiration for Kaitlin had grown every day, every minute, as she'd blossomed.

'Thank you—and thank you for all your support and understanding and love.'

'You have those for ever, Kaitlin.'

Her smile lit up her face as she gestured forward to the Bridge of Sighs. 'Then it is appropriate that we are here.'

'It's perfect timing, indeed.'

His heart thudded in anticipation as he reached into his pocket and pulled out a jewellery box. Not a doubt crossed his mind. Instead hope and love filled his heart as he flicked the lid open to reveal the ring he had designed himself—a twist of emerald, ruby and diamond that glinted in the wintry November sun.

'Lady Kaitlin Derwent—love of my life, the woman I want to wake up next to for the rest of my life—will you marry me?'

Joy tinged her expression and her green eyes sparkled with the happiness he knew to be reflected in his own.

'Daniel Harrington—love of my life, my rock, my best friend—I would be more than honoured.'

He slipped the ring on to her finger, and as they swept under the Bridge of Sighs he kissed her and knew that their love would indeed be eternal.

* * * * *

*If you loved this story,
then you won't want to miss
RAFAEL'S CONTRACT BRIDE
and
THE EARL'S SNOW-KISSED PROPOSAL,
the first two books in Nina Milne's*
THE DERWENT FAMILY *trilogy.
Available now!*

*If you want to read about
another wealthy hero, then try
BEHIND THE BILLIONAIRE'S GUARDED
HEART
by Leah Ashton.*

MILLS & BOON®
Large Print – September 2017

The Sheikh's Bought Wife
Sharon Kendrick

The Innocent's Shameful Secret
Sara Craven

The Magnate's Tempestuous Marriage
Miranda Lee

The Forced Bride of Alazar
Kate Hewitt

Bound by the Sultan's Baby
Carol Marinelli

Blackmailed Down the Aisle
Louise Fuller

Di Marcello's Secret Son
Rachael Thomas

Conveniently Wed to the Greek
Kandy Shepherd

His Shy Cinderella
Kate Hardy

Falling for the Rebel Princess
Ellie Darkins

Claimed by the Wealthy Magnate
Nina Milne

0817 Rom LP